#8

Feb 2018 - 1

Sue
R

Pride and Publishing

DeAnna Julie Dodson

AnniesFiction.com

Library of Congress-in-Publication Data
Pride and Publishing/ by DeAnna Julie Dodson
p. cm.
I. Title
           2017957486

AnniesFiction.com
(800) 282-6643
Secrets of the Castleton Manor Library™
Series Creator: Shari Lohner
Series Editor: Lorie Jones
Cover Illustrator: Jesse Reisch

10 11 12 13 14 | Printed in China | 9 8 7 6 5 4 3 2 1

"She's here."

Faith Newberry didn't have to ask her superior to clarify. For the past week, Marlene Russell—the assistant manager of Castleton Manor in Lighthouse Bay, Massachusetts—had talked of little else besides the arrival of Camilla Courtenay, the reigning queen of Regency romance at Northanger Press.

"I've already checked her suite," Marlene said, patting her perfectly coiffed blonde hair as she studied her reflection in one of the lobby mirrors. She was elegantly turned out as always.

"For the hundredth time," Brooke Milner muttered. She looked neatly turned out herself in her white chef's uniform.

Marlene fixed her with a poisonous glare. "I hope we've all taken special care in preparing for this event. If we give Ms. Courtenay and her dog the star treatment she expects, Northanger might schedule more of their events here."

At the last meeting of the Candle House Book Club, Faith had mentioned how worked up Marlene was over hosting Camilla Courtenay and Northanger's Regency Writing Contest and Fan Event. Faith had come to the conclusion that no-nonsense Marlene was a closet Regency romance reader and a fan of Camilla's work, and Brooke had confirmed it by saying Marlene had admitted to having all of Camilla's fifty-seven books. Most of them in hardcover.

Brooke shot Faith a smug look that said she remembered that conversation too, and Faith barely suppressed a smile.

"Now, you will have dinner ready on time, yes?" Marlene asked.

"Everything's right on schedule," Brooke assured her. "Straight off her list of favorites."

"And no peanuts," Marlene warned.

"No peanuts. No peanut oil. Nothing that's touched peanuts. I even took home all the peanut butter cookies I made this weekend."

Marlene appeared unamused. She turned to Faith. "The library?"

"All spruced up and ready for company," Faith said. "I made a display of the collection of Camilla's books that Northanger sent over last month. I think Camilla will be pleased."

"*Ms. Courtenay*," Marlene corrected her primly, "may not spend much time in the library, since this is meant to be more of a pleasure trip than work for her, but if she does pay you a visit there, please make sure everything is in order."

Faith glanced around the lobby they stood in, which gleamed in the sparkling glow of the chandeliers. Marlene had certainly done her part as far as seeing that the housekeeping staff had the entire manor looking its polished best.

Before Marlene could make any more demands, the front doors swung open, admitting several people. In the center of the group was a woman in her midfifties with bright blue eyes and snow-white hair that fell in poodle-like natural curls to her shoulders.

"Short, isn't she?" Brooke whispered to Faith.

Marlene gave them both a look that demanded silence or death, and then she put on her most welcoming smile as she glided across the lobby to greet the new arrivals. "Ms. Courtenay, it's wonderful to have you with us. And who is this?"

Faith could hardly believe it, but Marlene was actually cooing over the white teacup Pomeranian Camilla was carrying. Marlene had never expressed any interest in dogs—or any other animal for that matter, including Faith's black-and-white tuxedo cat, Watson—though the manor catered to pets and their owners.

The dog yipped at Marlene, making her flinch, but she managed to keep the smile on her face.

"This is Emma," Camilla said in a babyish voice, "and she's my honey pie, aren't you, Emmie? Aren't you? Aw, such a sweet girl."

The tiny dog wriggled and licked Camilla's face as Marlene looked on indulgently.

"We're so pleased to have you both," Marlene said, and then she nodded at the rest of the party. "Welcome to Castleton Manor."

"Oh, goodness," Camilla drawled, "my manners! This is Ralph Carlson." She took the arm of the tall balding man beside her. "He's my editor at Northanger. He and his team ensure that my stories make sense after I turn them in."

Marlene shook his hand. "Mr. Carlson."

"Ms. Russell," he said in a deep voice, "I'm glad to finally meet you. My assistant, Tony, told me you made his job extremely easy when he called to reserve the manor for our event."

"This is Tony," Camilla said, beaming at the young man at Ralph's side. "Isn't he darling? I must make him a count or a duke in one of my books, don't you think?"

Tony was good-humored enough to give her a smile and a slight bow in response. He seemed to be used to Camilla's admiration.

Faith had to admit that the tall, dark, and handsome young man with impossibly blue eyes would make a good romance novel hero. She glanced at Brooke, who obviously agreed, and gave her friend a subtle elbow to the ribs to let her know she was staring at him.

Brooke shot her a mischievous grin, then gazed demurely at the floor.

"Go on and look, honey," Camilla said to Brooke. "I keep telling Giselle it doesn't cost anything."

The twenty-something brunette next to her rolled her eyes. "Mother."

"This is your daughter?" Marlene asked. "I didn't realize . . ."

Camilla smiled at the young woman, then turned to Marlene. "She's not involved in the contest, but I thought it would be fun for the three of us girls to have a little getaway. I know it's a last-minute change. It's not going to be a problem, is it?"

Faith could tell Marlene was mentally scrambling.

"You say the three of you. We thought . . ." Marlene glanced expectantly toward the slight young woman with dishwater-blonde hair who stood behind Camilla with a purple velvet dog cushion, a silver bowl, and a much-chewed stuffed rabbit in her arms.

Camilla gave a dismissive wave. "Oh, not Jenny. Dear Jenny looks after us, but that's her job. I'm sure Tony arranged a room for her already. I meant me and Giselle and Emmie. You do have a pet spa, don't you? That was one of the main reasons we wanted to come here, wasn't it, Ralph?"

"I'm sure the manor can accommodate everyone," he assured her. "Isn't that right, Ms. Russell?"

"Certainly," Marlene told him. "We will prepare a suite for Miss Courtenay. And of course, we have our billiard room, a gym, and a crafts room as well as a number of outdoor activities available to all our guests. Little Emma can enjoy the pet spa and a special treat from Happy Tails Gourmet Bakery. We provide a small selection of their goodies here, but Emma might like taking a trip to the bakery for a wider variety."

Emma perked up and barked as if in agreement.

"In addition, the manor library has quite an extensive collection of books for all tastes." Marlene gestured to Faith. "This is our librarian, Faith Newberry. She can help with anything you need."

"So pleased to meet you, Ms. Courtenay," Faith said, stepping forward.

"Please call me Camilla. All of you."

Marlene's smile tightened slightly.

"It's good to have you at the manor," Faith said, acknowledging each of the guests. "And thank you, Mr. Carlson, for the set of Camilla's books you sent to the library. Our visitors will really appreciate them."

"Goodness, I hope so." Camilla shook her head. "I'd like to take some of those early ones and blow them up and start over, but I guess we all have to begin somewhere."

"I don't think you should change a thing," Faith told her. "I've been reading your books since I was in high school, and I've always enjoyed them. And I believe Ms. Russell has every one of them. I think she's one of your biggest fans."

Marlene colored and managed a faint smile.

"You are?" Camilla put one hand on the assistant manager's arm. "Oh, honey, I'd like to run you through my printer and make a couple million copies."

Faith could tell Brooke was fighting a grin.

Marlene gave Brooke a very cool stare. "You should tell Ms. Courtenay what you have planned for dinner tonight." She turned to the guests. "Brooke Milner is our sous-chef and is responsible for much of the meal planning."

"We wanted to make your first night here a special one," Brooke said, "so we're serving hazelnut salad with shiitake mushrooms. Then for the main course, we'll have chicken breasts with spinach and leeks in a brandy-mustard cream sauce, yam soufflé, and carrots al dente."

"Oh, lovely," Camilla said. "I don't like mushy carrots."

"And for dessert, we have blackberry pie in a teacup."

Camilla let out a blissful sigh. "You know, Ralph, I'm going to like it here. Emma and I may have to come back and stay awhile sometime later on."

"We'd be pleased to have you anytime," Faith said.

Marlene showed the guests up to their rooms, and Brooke and Faith headed to the kitchen.

"I have a feeling Camilla wasn't quite what Marlene expected," Brooke said as they walked down to the basement.

"Marlene did seem a bit put out when I mentioned she owns all of Camilla's books. I thought she'd be thrilled that her idol knew."

"Maybe Marlene expected someone British," Brooke suggested.

"Camilla is really good. She's definitely done her research on the Regency period and Jane Austen, and I'd bet she's read Georgette

Heyer too. Rakes and debutantes and elopements and marriages of convenience and duels. Lots of duels."

Brooke laughed. "I'm almost finished with *A Love Abandoned*. It's so romantic. I can't wait to discuss it tomorrow at our book club meeting."

"That's Camilla's first novel and my favorite," Faith said. "There's something very real about the characters and what they go through. They're rereleasing the book for its twenty-fifth anniversary, and the new edition will be unveiled on Friday night at the ball."

"I'll have to get a copy of the new edition. And I want to read more of her books. Which ones do you recommend?"

"You can't go wrong with any of them," Faith said automatically, then hesitated. "Actually, don't tell anyone I said so, but Camilla's last three or four have been sort of retreads. I guess it's hard to keep turning out fresh material two or three times a year."

Faith stopped when they reached the kitchen door. "Don't say anything, but I smuggled Aunt Eileen's first edition of the book out of her house last time I was there. I'm going to ask Camilla to autograph it, and I'm buying a copy of the new version so I can give them both to Eileen for her birthday."

Brooke smiled. "She'll love that. I know she's dying to meet Camilla anyway."

"I can't imagine why," said an icy voice behind them.

Faith and Brooke both turned to see Marlene coming down the stairs.

"Why would you say that?" Faith asked. "She's a big fan."

"Like you," Brooke added with the tiniest hint of a smirk.

"Don't you have a dinner to make?" Marlene snapped.

"Yes ma'am!" With a crisp salute, Brooke disappeared into the kitchen, leaving Faith and Marlene alone in the hallway.

"I thought you liked Camilla's books," Faith said.

"I've read them," Marlene admitted, her mouth in a tight line. "What I read led me to believe the author would be . . . special somehow."

"Now that's not fair. She seems very nice and friendly, and she's not at all pretentious. What did you expect? That she would have a British accent and drink tea all the time?"

"With those witty lines and high society affairs? I suppose I thought she'd be different. If I didn't know she was an American, I would think from reading her books that she was English."

"I'd say that means she's a gifted writer." Faith studied her for a moment. "Does it make any difference where she's from?"

"Don't be absurd. That doesn't matter to me in the least. I just came to tell you that Ms. Courtenay wants to know if the library has any books on English inheritance laws of the early 1800s. She's plotting out a new book and wants to do some research."

Faith nodded. "I'll find her something. What room did you give her?"

"The Jane Austen Suite of course. I had to do some shuffling, but I put her daughter next to her and the assistant on the other side of the daughter. Mr. Carlson's next to Ms. Courtenay in the Agatha Christie Suite and his assistant next to him. All that's left is to get the three contestants checked in."

"It must be quite an achievement for them to make it to the final round after five or six preliminary ones. I don't know how many thousands of writers entered the contest in the first place."

Marlene looked unimpressed. "I guess they have about as much chance of winning this contest as they would of being picked up off some agent's slush pile. Peculiar way of awarding a publishing contract, if you ask me."

"I think it's exciting."

"I don't understand why the contestants are coming now," Marlene went on, as if she hadn't heard Faith. "It's only Sunday. I know the winner will be announced at the ball on Friday, but what will they do the rest of the week?"

"Camilla's going to judge their final entries."

Marlene frowned. "She doesn't need them here to do that, does she? Besides, she's probably already chosen the winner. From what I saw, all she wants to do is lounge around the manor, eat gourmet food, and pamper that little white rat of hers."

Faith shook her head. "You don't have to dislike her because she isn't what you expected."

"I do not dislike her. I have no feelings about her in the least." Marlene pursed her lips. "Ms. Courtenay is a guest and will receive excellent service every moment she's at the manor. As all our guests do."

"Good. And as far as the contest is concerned, I understand she doesn't have any idea who the finalists are. She won't know until they're presented to her at dinner tonight. I suppose the publisher didn't want her to have any preconceived notions about them." Faith gave Marlene her sweetest smile. "You know what a nuisance those can be."

Marlene huffed. "Just take her the books she wants and see if there's anything else you can get her from the library. I'm going to make sure the contestants' rooms are ready."

Faith couldn't help but grin as Marlene marched up the stairs. She couldn't wait to meet the rest of their guests.

Dinner tonight was sure to be interesting.

Faith knocked on the door to the Jane Austen Suite and was immediately invited to come in.

Camilla was curled up on the pale gold brocade chaise longue in front of the bay window, with a stack of books on the floor behind her and her laptop open. Her face lit up when she saw her visitor. "Faith, it's so good to see you."

"I know you're getting settled in," Faith said, shutting the door behind her, "so I won't stay long. Ms. Russell told me you wanted something on English inheritance laws, and I'm sorry to say we don't have very much, but I thought this might help. It's from 1836." She handed Camilla a heavy book bound in cracked leather. Its embossed title was nearly worn away.

"Thank you. I can find most anything I need on the Internet, but some of these fiddly little questions aren't so easy to research without a real book." She motioned to a tufted oval-backed chair. "Please have a seat."

Faith looked around the room. Seeing no one else present but Emma, who was soundly asleep on her purple velvet cushion, Faith perched on the edge of the chair. "Unless it's a secret, I'd love to know what you're researching. How do you manage to come up with so many wonderful ideas?"

Camilla laughed softly. "A lot of it comes from researching the period. You know, what would *Pride and Prejudice* be without the legal complication of entailment? Jane could have inherited Longbourn and kept the whole family with her, and Lizzy would never have had to deal with that odious Mr. Collins."

Faith smiled. "I suppose you're right. Is that the sort of thing you're going to write about next?"

"Oh no. There's nothing I could add to what Miss Austen did. But I'm thinking there has to be some reason an older son could be disinherited in favor of the younger, and that would make some delicious tension between the boys, don't you think? I'll find out what the law used to say on the matter and go from there."

"I'm already intrigued," Faith admitted. "But don't you have enough to do this week with judging the contest and everything?"

"A writer is only as good as her last book. If I don't keep writing, keep publishing, keep topping whatever I did last, somebody else will take my place."

"I still think you're the queen of Regency romance."

Camilla smiled. "That will always be Georgette Heyer in my eyes, but thank you all the same."

Faith glanced around the ornate suite. "I thought your daughter might be in here with you."

"If I know Giselle, she's napping in her room." Camilla leaned closer and said in a confidential tone, "I think she's been sleeping too much these days. I told her she needs to get out in the sun and be around people instead of hiding in her room, but I hate to push too much. Especially after everything that's happened."

Faith didn't know what had happened, but she didn't want to pry, so she merely looked sympathetic.

"Oh, silly me." Camilla laughed lightly. "Here I am, talking like we're old friends already, and you don't know me from Adam's off ox. Some awful young man made my poor baby believe he loved her and then jilted her practically at the altar. Can you imagine? It's been almost three months now, and Giselle hasn't been the same since."

"I'm so sorry," Faith murmured.

"Not that Giselle couldn't have her pick. But she was absolutely crazy about him, engaged and everything, and suddenly he dropped her. Just like that. She's been crushed ever since. That's why I thought she ought to join me this week. To get away from everything. And strictly between you and me, I'm hoping she'll meet someone else. Maybe at the ball on Friday."

"We can at least try to make sure she has a good time," Faith said, knowing from personal experience that the last thing Giselle was likely to want was to be pushed into meeting someone before she was ready.

Camilla nodded. "I guess that's the most we can hope for." She thumbed through the book Faith had brought her. "This will give me a good place to begin. And I may take a nap myself in a little while. I want to be fresh and bright-eyed for dinner tonight. I'm dying to meet our three finalists. Ralph won't tell me a thing. He says I have to wait."

"It is mysterious. You don't know anything about the contestants?"

Camilla shook her white curls. "Not in the least. But the judges for the regional contests thought they were the best." She sighed. "I didn't get to read their entries, of course. I'm not supposed to have any preconceived notions about them. Even when I meet them, I shouldn't have any idea about how they write. It's meant to be a completely blind selection."

"Will it be the same entries they used for the regional contests? Or are they bringing something new for the final judging?"

Camilla's blue eyes sparkled. "That's the most intriguing part. They aren't bringing anything. They don't know what they'll be doing once they get here, and neither do I."

Faith grinned. "Oh, that sounds really interesting."

"Sneaky Ralph has it all planned out," Camilla continued. "They have until the morning of the ball to finish their entries, and then Ralph and I will spend the day reading them and choosing the winner. Naturally, he's going to be polite and say the choice was mine, but I know he wants to make sure I pick the right one. After all, he's the one who'll have to work with the winner after she signs the contract."

"I don't think I've ever heard of a writing contest quite like that. It sounds like a lot of work in such a short time."

"They might as well get used to it. If they're going to be in the business, they need to learn how to produce on a deadline."

"I guess that's true," Faith said, standing. "I'm sure we'll find out more about it at dinner."

"I'm glad you'll be there." Camilla stood too. "You'd think I'd be used to these events after twenty-five years or so, but I always get slightly nervous about them. You make me feel a little more at home."

Faith smiled at her. "I'll be there. And don't be nervous. Everybody will love being able to chat with you. And no matter what, Mr. Jaxon will soon make you feel like you've been friends for years."

"Wolfe Jaxon?" Camilla walked Faith to the door and opened it for her. "The owner of the manor, right?"

"Yes, and he's a very nice man." Faith gave her a conspiratorial smile. "He wouldn't make a bad hero for one of your books either."

Camilla grinned. "Then I am absolutely looking forward to tonight." With a small wave, she shut the door.

"Miss Newberry."

Faith quickened her step, surprised to see Ralph Carlson waiting for her outside the library door. "I'm so sorry. I was taking Camilla a book she wanted. I hope I haven't kept you waiting long."

"Not at all," he said, his smile warm. "I've been looking around down here. It's a beautiful place, just right for our event. I wanted to see what the library is like too while I have a minute."

"Of course." Faith unlocked the door and ushered him into the manor's two-story library.

"Excellent," he said, taking in the massive fireplace and the richly paneled walls and then the ceiling painted with a host of Renaissance angels. His eyes lit up when he noticed the special display of Camilla's books. "Camilla will be pleased to see this."

Faith had set out the books in order of publication on a Georgian rosewood side cabinet with a pair of the manor's antique porcelain figurines depicting a Regency gentleman and his lady. Beside the display was a stand with a large publicity photo of Camilla. Her hair was different now and she didn't look quite so young, but her smile and sparkling blue eyes hadn't changed.

"I hope everything is exactly the way you want it, Mr. Carlson," Faith said. "Let me know if anything isn't, and I'll see to it right away."

"Everything's perfect so far. And please call me Ralph. I have a feeling Northanger Press will be scheduling many more events here in the future, so we might as well dispense with the formalities."

"Thank you. Do call me Faith."

"All right, Faith. I just spoke to Tony, my assistant. He picked up the contestants from the airport, and they're on their way. If you have no objections, I think this would be the ideal place for me to meet them and let them know how the final round of the contest is going to work."

"That won't be a problem. Do you want me to arrange for refreshments?"

"That's an excellent idea. Maybe coffee and some kind of hors d'oeuvres? Nothing that will spoil dinner but enough to tide them over till then."

"Certainly. I'll speak to the sous-chef."

"Thank you." Ralph looked around the room again. "Would it be all right if we sat before the fireplace? I realize it's too warm for a fire, but it seems like a cozy place to gather. I want them all to relax and enjoy themselves tonight. Tomorrow the hard work begins."

"You're all very welcome. There'll be three of them?"

He nodded and pulled a small notebook out of the breast pocket of his suit jacket. "Melanie Wilde, winner of our Western region contest, Sarah Estelle Greenwich, winner in the East, and Angelique Desjardins, the Central winner."

Faith smiled. "They definitely sound like romance writers. I'm eager to meet them."

"I'm wondering if you might join us too," Ralph said. "They're probably going to use the library during their stay, and if you could show them around, explain how everything's laid out, and let them know you're here to help during the week, I'd very much appreciate it. We're going to be putting them under a good deal of pressure, and I want them to have the resources they need to do their best."

"I'm happy to help in any way I can."

"Thank you." He checked his watch. "I'd better go out to the lobby. Unless there was a traffic jam, Tony and the contestants ought to be arriving any minute now."

"I'll arrange the coffee and hors d'oeuvres, then meet you there."

A few minutes later, Faith was standing at Ralph's side when the front doors opened and Tony ushered in two women and a man.

Ralph gave his assistant a puzzled look.

Tony shrugged. "Mr. Carlson, this is Ms. Sarah Estelle Greenwich," he said, indicating the swarthy middle-aged woman on his left.

"Ms. Greenwich," Ralph said, "very good to meet you."

"Miss Melanie Wilde," Tony said with a slight bow of his head to the twenty-something with long, sun-bleached hair who stood on his other side.

The woman's long lashes swept to her cheeks under his gaze, but she said nothing.

"Miss Wilde," Ralph said graciously, but he still glanced questioningly at the man next to her.

The man was in his late twenties, Faith thought, professionally dressed and good-looking, though without Tony's cover-model handsomeness.

"And Ms. Desjardins?" Ralph asked. "Was there a problem, Tony?"

"Mr. Carlson," the man said, extending his hand, "I'm Angelique Desjardins."

3

Ralph stared at the man's outstretched hand and then his face, obviously bewildered.

The man chuckled. "Angelique Desjardins is my pen name. My real name is Alex Denning."

Laughing, Ralph finally shook his hand. "It's nice to meet you. Now allow me to introduce you all to Faith Newberry. She's the librarian here at the manor, and she's been kind enough to let us use the library to relax for a few minutes before you get settled in your rooms. Let's have some coffee and talk about what this week will be like for the three of you."

Taking her cue, Faith smiled and said, "If you'll follow me, the library is this way." She directed them to the sofas and chairs near the library fireplace.

Soon one of the staff arrived with coffee and Brooke's delicious smoked salmon crisps.

Before long, Ralph had everyone chatting about their work, and Faith couldn't help smiling to herself. Evidently the one sure way to get writers to talk was to bring up the subject of writing.

"The hardest thing," Melanie said, "is trying to come up with a story that's new and fresh while still fitting in the genre you want to write and giving readers the kind of story they're looking for."

Tony nodded sympathetically.

"You mean," Alex said with a sardonic grin, "something different but exactly like whatever's selling?"

Ralph laughed. "That's precisely what most publishers are searching for. I have to admit that you're a bit of a surprise, Alex. You don't look much like an Angelique."

"For that I am extremely grateful. But be honest. If I had put Alex Denning on a query, would you have given it a second look?"

Ralph appeared faintly uncomfortable. "Certainly. It's all about the quality of the writing and, of course, the story itself."

"And you would have assumed *Alex* was short for *Alexis* or *Alexandria*."

The editor shrugged. "I guess you're right. We just don't have many romance writers, especially Regency, who are men. Obviously, you know your stuff, or you wouldn't have gotten this far in the contest."

"But if you win," Melanie observed, sneaking a peek at Tony, "book signings are going to be a little awkward."

Alex smiled beatifically. "I'll worry about that after I sign my contract."

"Such children," the woman at Faith's left said good-humoredly, speaking for the first time. "I used to think it would be that easy when I started out too."

"Have you been writing a long time, Ms. Greenwich?" Faith asked.

"Call me Ann. Alex here isn't the only one who uses a pen name. My real name is Ann Giordano."

Ralph glanced at Tony. "I guess we're nearly as in the dark as Camilla is about our finalists."

"'What's in a name?'" Tony quoted philosophically. "People are who they are, no matter what we call them, don't you think so, Miss Wilde?"

Melanie nodded, trying but failing to look coolly impersonal.

Faith pretended she hadn't noticed the spark of attraction between the two of them.

"It comes out," Ann said, something glittering in her dark eyes. "The true nature will always come out eventually."

There was silence for a moment, and then Faith turned to Ann. "I'm sure it's helpful for a writer to be able to read people well. You never did say how long you've been writing."

"Since I was young, like those two," Ann said. "I had big plans and was determined to fulfill them. Then I found out how hard it is to make a living on nothing more than a dream." She sighed. "Ah, well, nobody wants to hear my tired old story. Let me just say that after a day's work as a secretary or an accountant or whatever pays the bills, it's not easy to go home and write the great American novel. Especially after you've done the shopping and cleaned the house and taken care of the yard and cooked dinner and a million other things."

"I suppose not," Faith said.

Melanie shrugged. "So you let your husband do most of that stuff."

"If you have one," Ann said crisply. "Otherwise you're on your own."

"Those are only the ones who aren't published yet," Alex said with a dismissive wave of one hand. "Once you get a book deal, there's no way but up from there."

Faith fought a smile. She wasn't a writer herself, but when she had worked as a librarian and archivist at Hawarden University, she had assisted a number of authors with their research. Except for the very few who made the best-seller lists, even the published ones had to work hard to keep getting contracts, hoping someday to write a book that really caught on. It was even harder for them to live off their writing income, especially without a patron or a spouse. Or a wealthy family.

"If I'd come from money," Ann said, her gaze sweeping over Melanie from her designer shoes to her diamond earrings, "it might not have taken me so long to get here."

Melanie turned faintly red, but she said evenly, "Money doesn't buy talent. Or hard work."

"It does buy convenience," Ann replied, her expression more wistful than censorious. "And free time."

"Free time is one thing none of you will have after tonight," Ralph said heartily. "I promise you that whoever wins this contest will have earned it."

The three hopefuls glanced at one another uncertainly.

"I won't reveal all the details quite yet," Ralph continued. "But I will let you know that once you find out what is expected of you in the morning, you'll be entirely on your own. No telephones. No Internet."

Faith managed not to look amused at Melanie's dumbfounded expression.

"You may ask either Tony or Faith for any research material you need." Ralph turned to Faith. "I hope you don't mind helping from time to time."

"Why, no," Faith said, surprised but not displeased by the unexpected request. "Not at all. I'll be happy to do whatever I can."

"And if any of you has a question that can't be answered by one of the books in the library," Ralph said, "Faith can research it for you on the Internet. Fair enough?"

Alex appeared irritated by the restrictions, but he nodded. "I guess as long as we're all in the same boat, it's okay." He eyed the two women he'd be competing against. "Keeps us honest."

"Fine by me," Ann said. "I did plenty of historical research long before there was an Internet. I only wish I had the rest of my research notebooks with me."

"We can call home, right?" Melanie asked. "My parents would worry if they didn't hear from me for nearly a week."

"You'd better call them tonight and tell them what's going on," Ralph said. "If you need to call later, you'll have to do it in my presence. The point here is that we want to know what each of you can do on your own under pressure. No outside help, no brainstorming, no commiserating. Nothing."

Nobody said a word.

"Anyone want to back out?" Ralph asked congenially. "No hard feelings."

"I'm game," Alex said. "Ladies?"

Melanie jutted out her chin. "I'm not quitting."

"Definitely not," Ann said.

Faith found it hard to concentrate on her regular work that afternoon. There were a few books in the library about Jane Austen's life and what it was like to live in Regency England, and she was tempted to read up on the period in order to be prepared. Faith didn't know what she might be called on to research before the week was over. Even though she had met Ralph only recently, she had already decided that he was the type of person to throw an unexpected twist into a contest like this.

Finally, when it was almost closing time, she gave in to temptation and skimmed through a book on Regency slang. By the time she locked the library door, she was sure that if any of the contestants wanted to research a story about "a corky pink of the ton who was so tap-hackled he mistakenly got leg shackled to an ape-leader who had never a feather to fly with," she would definitely be able to help. The thought made her laugh.

"Well, you ought to let us in on the joke."

She turned to see Camilla smiling at her. Jenny, her assistant, stood behind her holding Emma.

Faith grinned. "I've been reading up on the cant terms they used in the elite circles in England two hundred years ago. Some of them are pretty amusing."

"Aren't they?" Camilla's bright eyes twinkled. "I love using those terms in my books. They give such a nice period feel to a story, and as you say, they're pretty amusing too."

Faith reached over to touch the pink bow on top of the little dog's head. "Aren't you looking lovely today, Emma?"

The Pomeranian yipped happily in response.

"We've both been to the spa," Camilla said. "I wanted to look especially nice for tonight, and I didn't think it was fair for Emma not to get her turn too. I tried to get Giselle to join us, but she didn't feel up to it." She turned to her assistant. "Jenny got a bit of pampering as well."

Jenny smiled shyly and displayed her French manicure.

"I hope you're enjoying your stay so far," Faith said to her.

Jenny nodded. "Camilla always goes to the nicest places. I'm lucky to be able to come along."

"Dear Jenny looks after us so wonderfully," Camilla gushed. "Doesn't she, Emmie sweetie? We absolutely couldn't do without her, could we?"

Jenny turned slightly pink and busied herself with Emma's bow.

"Will you be at dinner tonight?" Faith asked her.

Jenny blinked. "Uh, no ma'am. I mean, somebody has to look after Emma and everything, because dinner will probably go on past her bedtime."

Camilla nodded solemnly.

"Ah," Faith said, not quite sure how to respond to that, since she'd never heard of a dog with a bedtime. "And your daughter?" she asked Camilla.

"Giselle isn't interested in 'a stupid business meeting, thank you very much,'" Camilla said with her usual good humor. "But I imagine she'll be feeling a bit more sociable tomorrow. Travel never suits her, but she gets over it quickly."

Jenny checked her watch. "Did you and Emma still want to have a nap before dinner?"

"Yes, of course. I want to be rested and at my best when I finally get to meet our mysterious finalists." Camilla laid one hand on Faith's arm. "You're still coming, aren't you?"

"Ralph said he wanted me to come," Faith said. "And Mr. Jaxon will be there too, I believe. I for one am eager to know what you think of the contestants."

Camilla's eyes widened. "You've met them! Oh, you have, haven't you?"

Faith nodded, smiling. "Ralph met with them in the library when they got in. I believe they're supposed to be staying in their suites and out of sight until they're officially presented to you at dinner."

Camilla glanced around and then leaned closer. "What are they like?"

Faith shook her head. "You'll have to wait and see."

One of the best things about being feline, the cat considered, was the amazing number and variety of interesting playthings available everywhere. The manor had humans coming and going all the time, bringing their dogs and cats and sometimes rabbits and birds and such, so there was always something new to see or smell or taste and something different to explore. His favorites were the easily provoked little dogs who sometimes came to visit. There was one in the manor now, and he wanted to see if he could set it off without getting in trouble with his human. She was always lecturing him about leaving the silly things alone, even though he never actually did anything to any of them.

It wouldn't hurt, though, to find out what he could before his human came home. He didn't want to miss his dinner, especially if she remembered to bring him some tunaroons. They were better than teasing a hundred dogs—well, maybe fifty. But there was no reason he couldn't have both, was there? He was a cat after all.

He made his way unseen into the manor and up to the second floor where the new humans would be sleeping. Yes, there was definitely a dog. It had been in at least three of the rooms, but it was somewhere else now. Good. He didn't want it to start yapping and alerting any humans to his presence. There was too much to check out first.

He was rather disappointed once he had investigated all the occupied guest rooms. Besides the dog, which he had only caught scent of so far, there wasn't all that much worth his notice. One of the humans had a long necktie hanging over the back of a chair, and, of course, it was his duty as a cat to make sure that it ended up on the floor. Another one had some white stuff in a pump bottle, and he licked the residue off the outside. As always, he couldn't believe humans preferred to rub this on their skin instead of eating it.

In another room, he found a long piece of ribbon like the ones his human sometimes put in her hair, and he spent an entertaining minute or two pretending he was chasing a fluttering butterfly. He pushed a pencil around on a table in a different room, chewed the sharpened end until the lead was showing nicely, and swatted it into a nearby wastepaper basket with a satisfying thump.

That made the cat wonder what else might be in the basket, so he leaped inside and poked around, but it was practically empty. He'd have to come back after the humans had been here a little longer if he wanted to find anything interesting. When he jumped out, he noticed something white under the bed. Immediately on alert, he crouched down and slunk toward it. It was only a crumpled piece of paper, but it was just the right size to bat all over the floor and then carry off in his mouth afterward.

Once he had finished investigating the guests, he made his way over to the big room with all the books where his human usually was. He could see her down on the first floor with three of the other humans and, yes, the dog. It was one of those very tiny ones that yipped at everything. It would be a lot of fun.

Still carrying his crumpled paper, the cat trotted downstairs to get a closer look at the visitors. By the time he got there, they were gone and had taken the dog with them. His human had left her purse behind, though.

It seemed like a nice time to enjoy a nap in the sun, so he dropped his paper ball into the purse for safekeeping and headed out to the warm grass.

It had been a good morning.

Faith walked through the Victorian garden toward the stone cottage that had once been inhabited by the manor's gardener. Living there with the sounds and smells of the ocean around her was one of the best perks of her job, and she always felt especially blessed when she came home to it after a long day. As she reached her door, she heard a familiar meow from overhead.

"Watson." She put her hands on her hips. "What are you doing up there?"

The tuxedo cat lounged on the edge of the roof above the front door, enjoying the pleasant June weather and watching the twittering sparrows.

"How did you get out anyway? I thought I left you inside this morning. Have you been snooping in the manor again?"

Watson blinked his bright green eyes, looking rather smug. He showed no sign of coming down.

With a sigh, Faith reached into the roomy depths of her purse for her keys.

By the time she opened the door, Watson was at her feet, rubbing against her ankles and purring at maximum volume.

"You remembered it's time to eat, I see."

He made a satisfied, rumbly mew and bolted inside, heading straight for the kitchen, his bobbed tail quivering with excitement. He came back to the door, protesting as she stopped to kick off her shoes. It didn't matter that there was always food in his bowl and he could eat anytime. Faith's return at the end of the day was An Event, and the proprieties must be observed.

Once she had appeased Watson with a freshly opened packet of tuna-crab blend, Faith went to her bedroom to get ready for dinner. She slipped out of the outfit she had worn all day, removed and reapplied her makeup, and styled her chestnut locks. When she opened her closet door, she paused to admire the ivory silk gown that hung there, but it was for the ball on Friday. For tonight, she put on a shimmery blouse of peacock blues and greens and a pair of dressy black pants.

"You can stay home tonight then," she told Watson when he came to sit on her dresser to watch her put on her jewelry.

He gave her a look that clearly said, "Yeah, right."

"At least stay out of trouble. And in case you were wondering, the Pomeranian staying this week isn't coming to dinner either. Not this time anyway. If you behave, maybe you can meet her next time you visit the manor."

Watson appeared mildly annoyed, but she was fairly certain that was because he would not be allowed to tease the little dog once they were introduced.

Faith stood in front of her floor-length mirror to make sure she was properly put together. There was nothing in her reflection that even the immaculate Marlene could sneer at, not even cat hair on her black pants. Watson was ideal as far as the equitable distribution of noticeable cat hair was concerned, since he had black fur for her dark clothes and white fur for her light ones, but she had foiled him by dressing at the very last minute.

"No stray fur tonight," she said, giving him a pat right above his stubby tail.

Watson jumped off the dresser and followed her to the front door, purring and attempting to rub against her legs as she walked.

Somehow she escaped un-furred and hurried back through the garden toward the inviting lights of Castleton Manor.

Faith reached the lobby just as Wolfe Jaxon was coming down the stairs. As always, he looked flawless from his freshly cut dark hair sprinkled with gray to his charcoal-colored suit with fine pinstripes and all the way down to his custom-made Italian shoes.

He smiled when he saw her and quickened his step. "Good evening. Don't you look lovely."

"Thank you," Faith said, feeling her cheeks warm.

He opened the banquet hall door for her and followed her inside. Ralph and Tony were already at the table, talking to the three finalists over coffee. Tony was sitting next to Melanie.

Faith quickly introduced Wolfe to everyone. They joined the others at the table, and Wolfe poured coffee for Faith and himself.

A few minutes later Faith turned to Ralph. "Camilla said she was planning on taking a nap before dinner. She didn't oversleep, did she?"

"Oh no. She wouldn't miss an important occasion like this, and if she did, Jenny's there to remind her." He checked his watch. "It's not quite the hour yet."

The antique clock over the banquet room's fireplace showed one minute till.

Tony glanced at his boss. "Perhaps I should go up and see if she's coming."

Before Ralph could answer, the banquet hall door swung open and Camilla bustled inside. Her hair was teased into a soft white cloud around her head, a dramatic contrast to her shimmering black pantsuit and jet earrings and necklace. Her bright blue eyes sparkled as usual.

"Am I late?" she asked breathlessly, hands fluttering.

The antique clock gave a low chime in answer.

"Right on the dot," Ralph said.

The gentlemen stood, and Ralph pulled out Camilla's chair for her.

"I'm so sorry to have kept everyone waiting." She took her seat, smiling at everyone present as Ralph filled her cup for her. "I scared myself to death a minute ago, and my poor heart's still going a mile a minute."

"You didn't lose Emma, did you?" Faith asked.

"No, thank goodness. But from the way she was barking, I think she got a good scare too."

Everyone appeared faintly amused.

But Wolfe's expression also held a touch of concern. "I'm Wolfe Jaxon, the owner of Castleton Manor. I hope there's nothing wrong."

"I'm so pleased to meet you." Camilla extended her hand to him. "You were right," she told Faith in a confidential tone that everyone at the table could hear. "He'd make a fine hero in one of my books. *The Disinherited Duke? The Elusive Earl?* What do you think?"

Certain her face was burning, Faith did not look at Wolfe. "Uh, yes. Of course."

"That's very flattering, I'm sure," Wolfe said. "Still, if there's a problem, I want to see that it's put right."

Camilla laughed lightly. "Don't worry. As I said, it was only a scare. I spooked myself more than anything."

"What happened?" Wolfe pressed.

"Well, I was getting ready to come down here," Camilla said, "and I went into the bathroom to look in the mirror. I thought it would help if I switched on the lamp on the counter. It's a darling little thing. I think it's a Tiffany. Anyhow, I flipped on the switch, and what do you think happened?" Her eyes widened. "Why, there was a pop and a sizzle, and the light went out. For a second, I thought I had been electrocuted."

4

"Electrocuted?" Faith stared at Camilla. "Are you sure you're all right?"

"Oh yes, I'm fine," Camilla answered. "It was only a scare, like I said. No harm done in the least."

"I'm sorry," Wolfe told her, his handsome face grave as he set down his coffee cup. "That sort of thing can be very dangerous. I'll send someone up to replace the lamp right away."

"Now, don't fuss," Camilla said, then looked at her editor as if she were a naughty child. "And, Ralph, don't you worry either. Jenny's already seen to it. I think she was scared worse than anybody, what with me whooping and Emma barking like crazy. It was really kind of funny in hindsight."

"I can imagine," Faith said, relieved that nothing serious had happened.

"Anyway, she got one of the housekeepers to take the lamp away and bring in a new one, and everything is really—" Camilla stopped herself, as if suddenly remembering the rest of the people at the table. "I do apologize. We're certainly not here to talk about a silly old lamp." She regarded the contestants sitting across the table from her, then addressed Ralph. "You must introduce me. I thought there were supposed to be three of them. Where's the third?"

Alex, sitting in between Ann and Melanie, gave her a sly smile.

"You?" Camilla put one hand over her heart. "I assumed you were that young lady's husband or something."

"Nope," Alex said. "Just a humble writer of Regency romances."

"I think you'd better do the introductions, Ralph," Camilla said. "Before I make more embarrassing assumptions."

"We have Alex Denning, who writes as Angelique Desjardins. This is Ann Giordano, who writes as Sarah Estelle Greenwich."

Camilla looked at Ann oddly.

Seemingly unperturbed, Ann smiled in return and sipped her coffee. "And Melanie Wilde," Ralph continued, "who doesn't use a pen name." "Why would she?" Tony put in. "She has the perfect name already."

"I'm glad to meet you, Ms. Courtenay," Melanie said politely. "It's a real honor."

"Oh, please call me Camilla. All of you. There's no need for formality here. We're merely writers trying to get along in a tough business."

"I'm so happy to be here." Ann's enigmatic smile remained in place. "At last."

"And you, Alex," Camilla said swiftly, turning to him. "How in the world did you come to write Regency romance of all things?"

He shrugged. "I was a literature major for a while, and then, um, someone I knew left a romance book at my place, and I picked it up. I told her it was bad—I mean, really bad. Badly written, badly plotted, badly characterized. She said she liked it and bet me I couldn't do better. So I took her up on the bet and found out I had a pretty good time with it. I read some Georgette Heyer, and she seemed to have so much fun with her characters and the language they used and the social niceties of the time that I decided to give it a shot. I enrolled in some fiction writing classes, won a couple of local contests, took a few more classes, and then decided to try for a contract with Northanger. And here I am."

"That's a wonderful story," Camilla told him. "Goodness knows we can use some fresh blood in the genre and heroes who are real men and not tyrants or lapdogs." She put one hand on Faith's arm. "Don't tell Emma I said that."

Faith grinned and put a finger to her lips.

"What about you, Melanie?" Camilla asked. "Have you always wanted to be a writer?"

"I didn't know for a long time, to tell the truth." She pushed a lock of blonde hair behind one ear, obviously pretending not to notice that

Tony's gaze was on her. "I wanted to be everything from a ballerina to a brain surgeon when I was growing up, but then I started writing stories because I wasn't finding the kinds of books I wanted to read. I know a lot of people don't think storytelling is an important job, but I do."

"I think that's reason enough to do it." Wolfe smiled at her and then at Ann. "You haven't told us much about yourself yet. Have you been writing for a long time?"

There was humor in Ann's black eyes. "A very long time. Since I was in grade school. I wrote stories for my friends and stories with the characters from my favorite books and stories for television shows I liked. I thought I would become an author when I got out of college, but it took me a little longer than I imagined. I'm sure Camilla remembers how it was before she got her first contract."

Camilla smiled stiffly.

"Anyway," Ann said, "I'm hoping this contest will be my big break."

"That's what we're here for, right?" Ralph put down his coffee cup and tented his fingers on the table. "So who wants to know what this last round will involve?"

"I certainly do," Camilla said. "Knowing you, it'll be diabolical."

Ralph chuckled. "Only a little. Now here's the plan. We already know from the earlier rounds that the three of you can write, but we need to make sure you can write under pressure and still turn out something good. And we want to know that each of you was solely responsible for your earlier entries."

"How do we prove that?" Alex asked.

"Like I said earlier, first thing tomorrow morning, you'll have to surrender your phones and any other electronics that have Internet access," Ralph said. "The manor Wi-Fi will be password protected, so you won't have access through your laptops. The telephones in your suites are good only for reaching the front desk and room service. Once we have all the technology accounted for, you will each get a list of several Regency story elements. From that, you'll have to create a synopsis for a book that incorporates those elements and write a sample first chapter. You'll have until nine o'clock Friday morning."

Ann and Melanie glanced at each other.

"Whoa," Alex said under his breath.

Camilla clasped her hands together. "Oh, what fun! I'm glad I'm only the judge and not a contestant. I'm such a slow writer, especially these days, that I'm sure you'd all leave me in the dust."

Ralph gave her shoulder a fond pat. "You don't need to worry about that now. You just relax until Friday, and once you've picked a winner, all you'll have to do is dance the night away at the grand ball."

"That's right," Wolfe said graciously. "It's up to us at Castleton Manor to make sure you have a good time."

"I do love being catered to," Camilla said with a wink, and then, seeing Ann watching her, she sobered and said no more.

After dinner, Wolfe suggested a game of billiards, and the other men accepted, leaving Faith, Camilla, Melanie, and Ann still at the table.

"Are you sure you wouldn't like to play?" Faith asked them. "There are other games too, if you want something different."

"Not me," Melanie said, standing. "If you'll excuse me, I have to get out of these shoes." She displayed a slender foot in a strappy stiletto heel at least five inches high.

Faith winced in sympathy. "You're braver than I am."

Melanie wished them all good night, then left the banquet hall.

Once she was gone, Faith was more aware than ever of the tension between Ann and Camilla. It was almost as if Ann resented Camilla, but why? Just because Camilla was wildly successful and Ann was still striving to get her first contract? Or did they have some kind of history?

"It looks like you're going to have a busy week," Camilla ventured. "It does sound like fun, though. I always enjoy a real challenge."

"We could trade places," Ann offered, her tone light yet somehow cold.

Camilla's laugh was hollow. "That might be hard to arrange. You know, Anna—" She stopped herself and glanced at Faith. "Ann. You know everyone struggles starting out and almost constantly after that too. Even the newbies whose first books are runaway best sellers have to try to duplicate that success again and again and again. It's never easy. Not even fifty-something books later."

There was disdain in Ann's expression. "I'd like to at least have a chance at it."

"You've earned your chance now," Faith said, trying to make the conversation a little more cheerful. "You had to beat out an awful lot of people to get this far. I'd say that's an accomplishment in itself."

"I don't count on anything until it's actually done," Ann replied. "Things can turn completely around and blindside you at the last minute." She gave Camilla an acid smile. "Ask me how I know."

"Anna," Camilla breathed.

"You two know each other," Faith blurted out, and then she slapped one hand over her mouth. "I'm so sorry. It's really none of my business."

"Oh, don't worry about it, honey," Camilla said. "It's not a big deal. Yes, Ann and I know each other. *Knew* each other, I should say. It's been a long time, and everything's all blown over now, right?"

"The past is too heavy a burden to carry for long," Ann said archly. "I only hope you will give my entry a fair reading."

"For one thing, after twenty-five years, I wouldn't know your entry from anyone else's," Camilla said. "Even if I did, I wouldn't keep you from winning just because of—well, water under the bridge." Her expression suddenly turned winsome and appealing. "You do believe me, don't you?"

Ann's expression softened infinitesimally. "All right. I think I do anyway."

"I promise I'll pick the best entry, no matter whose it is." Camilla smiled mischievously. "Besides, Ralph will be looking over my shoulder the whole time, so what else can I do?"

Ann got to her feet. "Well, tomorrow is going to be busy, so I think I'll say good night too."

"I'm sorry," Faith said when she and Camilla were alone. "I didn't mean to pry. Or open up old wounds."

"Think nothing of it. I guess Ann and I must have blown things way out of proportion over all these years, and it's time we both realized that neither of us is the Wicked Witch of the West."

Faith couldn't help wondering what the two of them had quarreled over in the past and which one had wronged the other, but she told herself very strictly that she was not going to be intrusive. It was definitely none of her business.

"I'm glad the two of you got a chance to have a few words," Faith said. "Ann seemed a little more relaxed when she left a minute ago."

"I meant it. I'm going to pick the best entry, no matter what. I'm not going to punish her for some foolishness that was over years ago." Camilla yawned, putting a hand over her mouth. "Please excuse me. Despite my nap, I guess I need to get to bed. And I ought to go say good night to the gentlemen in the billiard room."

Faith nodded.

"Though I wouldn't be surprised to see that Melanie just happened to find her way over there as well." Camilla grinned as she stood. "She and Tony do seem to have a spark between them, don't they?"

"It does sort of look that way."

"I told you he'd make a fine hero for one of my books. The little rascal has already made a conquest."

"I don't know," Faith admitted. "Melanie seems determined to not let him distract her."

"I'd say she's doing a fair job of distracting him."

That made them both laugh.

"I don't suppose she'll have much time for him until the ball Friday night," Faith said.

"Mark my words," Camilla assured her. "They'll figure out something. She has to eat, doesn't she? Ten to one, they'll at least sit next to each other at dinner every night." With a grin, she disappeared into the corridor.

Faith watched after Camilla, wondering once more about her history with Ann. Could whatever grudge Ann was carrying against Camilla really be dismissed as easily as it seemed?

5

Faith had just gotten settled in the library the next morning and was pulling out some books on Regency dress when she heard a soft tap on the open door. She looked up to see Camilla's daughter, Giselle, peering into the room.

"It's huge." Giselle stared at the two levels of bookshelves and the frescoed ceiling high above. She had dark hair and was a head taller than Camilla, but with those bright blue eyes and that pert nose, no one would mistake them for anything but mother and daughter.

"It is," Faith agreed. "Won't you come in?"

With a glance behind her, Giselle rushed across the library to the shelf Faith was searching, almost running, as if she feared being caught.

"Is there something I can help you with?" Faith asked when the young woman didn't say anything. "I believe your mother's editor and the three finalists are coming down in a few minutes so they can get started on their entries."

"Right," Giselle said. "Mother told me, so I thought if I was going to get something to read, I'd better do it now."

"Good idea. What kind of books do you like? There's contemporary romance in that section over there. Historical right next to that. If you like Re—"

"Ugh. If you suggest Regency romance, I'll scream. I will absolutely scream right here in this library."

"Our books on structural engineering are on the third shelf from the corner over there," Faith said, not missing a beat.

Giselle laughed, looking relaxed for the first time. "Okay, that might be a little too serious. And boring. What about a nice cozy mystery? Nothing gory. Something fun. I mean, besides the murders and stuff."

Faith nodded. "We have many of those to choose from. Margery Allingham, Ngaio Marsh, Dorothy L. Sayers, Lilian Jackson Braun. We even have a complete set of Agatha Christie's works, first editions, autographed, though we don't lend those out."

"That's a nice collection," Giselle said, looking around the room again.

"Or do you prefer contemporary mysteries?"

"No, I like the old-fashioned ones," Giselle replied. "There's plenty of 'contemporary' around. I'd rather read about another time. And mysteries—well, it's nice to see the bad guys end up with what they deserve. Even if jerks get away with anything they want in real life."

"That is one of the nice things about the genre," Faith said. "There's so much that happens in life that doesn't make sense. But in a mystery when something awful happens, the truth comes out and the guilty are made to answer for what they've done. That is satisfying."

"I think you're right. Do you have—?"

"Gizi?"

Giselle froze.

Faith looked back and saw Alex Denning approaching them.

"Giselle," he said, appearing anxious.

Giselle's spine stiffened. Then she pasted on a smile and turned around. "Alex, I didn't expect to see you here."

"I didn't expect to see you here either. I thought you hated going on your mother's publicity tours."

"I do. I guess coming this time was a pretty lame idea after all." She looked him up and down. "Considering."

"Look—"

"I know you're about to have your big meeting with Mother and Ralph, so I'd better get going." Giselle snatched up a book, obviously at random. After what she had told Faith earlier, there was no way she could have meant to take Georgette Heyer's *Regency Buck*. "Now that you have what you want, don't mess it up." Head high and back ramrod straight, she marched out of the library.

Alex cringed. "That went well."

Faith gave him a sympathetic look. So Camilla wasn't the only one who had a history with one of the finalists. Of course, if this was the cad who had recently jilted her daughter, the history would be Camilla's too.

"I think I'm a little early," Alex said with a wry smile.

"The early bird gets the worm," Faith reminded him.

"Yeah, and the second mouse gets the cheese," he retorted.

As much as Faith would have loved to know the whole story between him and Giselle, it was none of her business. She decided to change the subject. "Are you ready to find out what your story elements will be?" she asked, assuming the topic was safe enough.

"That was the only thing I could think about last night," Alex admitted, and then he glanced at the door. "I'm glad that's all I had on my mind."

She settled him at the table with a cup of coffee and one of Brooke's cream cheese muffins. "I'm pretty curious myself. They're not giving the three of you much time to come up with your plot and characters."

"That's what makes it a challenge." Again Alex glanced at the door. "I just didn't expect to get my own special added element of stress." He sighed. "It must be obvious that Giselle and I know each other. Or did know each other."

Faith nodded, not sure how to respond.

"We dated for a while," Alex went on, "but I didn't meet Camilla until last night. She was on a European tour or something when Giselle and I started getting serious. But then again, Camilla seemed to be off somewhere or other the whole time I was seeing Giselle. It's probably a good thing we never met each other's families since it didn't work out anyway."

"I'm sorry."

For the third time Alex glanced at the door. "Since it really has nothing to do with the contest, maybe it would be best if Camilla didn't know about me and her daughter. That's over and done with. But I wouldn't want Camilla to discount my entry because of what happened with Gizi. Or bad-mouth me to Ralph. It most likely wouldn't take much. Publishing is a relatively small world. Somebody with Camilla's influence could make it difficult for someone like me if she wanted to."

"I won't breathe a word," Faith replied.

Before she could say anything else, Melanie and Ann walked through the door.

"Oh, that's exactly what I need." Melanie poured herself a cup of coffee, loaded it with cream and sugar, snatched up a muffin, and sat down. "I'm starving, but I didn't think I should eat a real breakfast. Too nervous."

Ann poured herself a cup of coffee too and took a seat across from Melanie.

Soon after, the rest of the expected party came in, Ralph with Camilla at his side, Tony following them with three large white envelopes under one arm, and Jenny at the rear, carrying Emma on her purple cushion. The dog glanced around and then yipped at something in the far corner of the library. Faith didn't see anything there.

"Hush now, Emmie," Camilla said, "or you'll have to go back upstairs."

"Shh," Jenny soothed her tiny charge, and Emma licked her face.

"I know I should have left her up in my suite," Camilla said, "but I wanted Jenny here just in case I needed something, and I couldn't leave poor Emma in that big room all by her little self, so here she is." She smiled at Ralph. "She promises to behave."

"I'm sure she will," Ralph said indulgently.

Faith noticed Melanie watching Tony as he got coffee for Camilla and Ralph, then served Jenny and himself.

Melanie must have realized that she was staring because she reddened slightly and said, "Are those envelopes what I think they are?"

Ralph nodded. "Those are your contest packets. They'll tell you everything you need to know for your entry—word count for your first chapter, synopsis requirements, and five elements that must be included in your story. Before you get to see them, you'll all have to give me your cell phones and anything else that will let you contact the outside world."

Melanie had a smartphone. Alex had two smartphones and a tablet. Ann had only an outdated cell phone.

"Very good," Ralph said as he collected the devices. "Now each of you give me your solemn promise you don't have anything of this nature you haven't told me about."

The three of them nodded, and Ralph looked significantly at Camilla.

"Thank you." Camilla smiled benevolently at the finalists. "I only wanted to say—"

The Pomeranian began to bark furiously, still staring at the far corner of the room, and Jenny shushed her.

"I'm so sorry, everyone," Camilla said. "Emma, shh. Come on now."

Emma quieted, but she continued to look in the corner.

Everyone focused on the dog. But Faith, suddenly realizing what was going on, glanced at the corner. She didn't see anything, but that didn't necessarily mean she was wrong.

"Now, Emmie, you be a good girl, or we won't get to visit that pet bakery Ms. Russell was telling us about."

Happy Tails Gourmet Bakery was always popular with the canine and feline visitors to the manor. Watson loved the tunaroons that were the bakery's specialty. He definitely wasn't going to get any today if he was doing what she thought he was.

"Thank you, sweetie." Camilla patted the dog's fluffy head and then turned to the contestants again. "I wanted to tell you all what I'm looking for in your entries. Everything Ralph already said, of course, but what I think would put one of you over the top is if you can surprise me." She smiled. "Now there are good surprises and bad surprises. Don't put something in there just because it's different."

"No cell phones," Alex deadpanned.

Camilla laughed. "I'm sure you all know that readers of Regency romance have certain expectations, and if you don't meet those expectations, no matter how gloriously written your story is, you will disappoint them. We don't want to disappoint them."

"But we do want to surprise them," Melanie said.

"Yes, we do."

"So something different," Alex said, "but exactly the same."

Camilla nodded. "Because that's really the only way you'll be able to please your audience. When I first started—"

Without warning, Emma leaped to her feet and began barking again.

This time Faith was quick enough to spot a pair of green eyes and a little pink nose peeping out from under the French bombé chest where she kept the library's office supplies. There would definitely be no tunaroons for Watson today.

Jenny picked up the dog and her cushion. "I'll take her into the garden for a walk."

"That's probably a good idea," Faith said. She'd deal with Watson later.

"I think we're about done anyway," Ralph said affably, and then he nodded at Tony, who passed out the envelopes to the contestants.

"You know from your earlier entries the kind of thing Northanger is looking for," Ralph continued. "You three have already impressed our judges with your storytelling abilities, but this is your last chance to show us your very best. Make it hard for us not to choose your entry." He stood, and everyone stood with him. "Take your packets and get to work. You have until nine on Friday morning to turn in your entries, complete or not. By Friday night, one of you will have a three-book contract with Northanger Press."

"Good luck," Camilla said, smiling at Melanie and then at Alex. "Good luck." Then she touched Ann's arm. "Good luck to you too."

Ann replied with a serene nod before following her fellow finalists out of the library.

Camilla turned to Ralph. "Is there anything else I need to do now?"

"Not till Friday morning. You and Emma enjoy yourselves and leave everything to me."

"And dear Tony, of course."

Tony nodded, smiling. "We'll see to everything."

Camilla sighed. "I wish Giselle wasn't so grumpy. Why pine over that ridiculous man she lost when there's a much better one right here?"

"I'm sure your daughter knows her own mind, ma'am," Tony said. "And after all, 'ladies' fancies must be consulted.'"

Faith recognized the quote from a Sherlock Holmes story, and evidently so did Camilla.

"Handsome *and* well-read?" she said to Faith in a stage whisper. "I'm sure some lucky young woman will snap him up before too long. And she might be right under his nose." She glanced over to the chair Melanie had just vacated.

Tony colored slightly.

"All right," Ralph said, subtly turning Camilla toward the door, "we should all clear out and let Faith get back to her real job. She's likely to have her hands full with research assistance over the next few days. Camilla, you'd better make sure Jenny hasn't lost Emma in that huge garden behind the manor."

Camilla's eyes widened. "Oh, dear. Excuse me."

"That's Camilla," Ralph said with a chuckle once she had hurried out of the room. "She wants everyone to have a happy ending."

"That's sweet of her," Faith said and then she looked hopefully at Tony. "You don't mind, do you?"

He shook his head. "I know she means to be complimentary. She's really a dear."

Faith smiled. He had a charming, old-fashioned way about him. No wonder Camilla pictured him as one of her romantic heroes.

"Thanks again, Faith, for hosting our meeting," Ralph said. "Let me know if you have any questions about what you can and can't do to help our contestants. The main thing is don't provide them with access to the Internet or a telephone. Give them all the research books they want, and feel free to look up specific questions for them."

"Got it," Faith said. "I'm looking forward to it. I've never been in on the creation of a plot for a novel before."

"I think you'll enjoy it. I saw these contestants' entries in the regional round. They're all excellent. Regardless of who wins, I think the three of them have potential in the publishing world. Come on, Tony. I have those galleys to look over, and I need you to set up that West Coast trip we were discussing. We'll talk to you later, Faith."

"Thanks," Tony said to Faith.

The two men walked out, debating whether the Four Seasons or The Garland would be the best venue for Camilla's next gala appearance.

Once Faith was sure they were gone, she strode over to the chest in the corner and dropped to her knees. "I know you're under there." She peered underneath and once more caught sight of the green eyes and pink nose she had seen before.

But he immediately retreated into the darkness farther back toward the wall.

"I know what you were doing." Faith reached under the chest until she caught hold of a struggling, furry somebody who most certainly did not want to be removed. She removed him anyway. "I told you that you were not to tease Camilla's dog."

Watson blinked at her, admitting nothing.

"Oh, don't give me that." Faith stood with him securely in her arms. "I saw you peeking out at her, letting her see you only long enough to get all worked up and then disappearing when anyone else looked." She had to force herself not to giggle at his disdainful expression. Clearly, he expected her to believe he was above such antics.

"No tunaroons for you, mister. And if I see you doing anything to upset Emma again, I'll have to keep you at home until she's gone. That's nearly a week. Do you realize that?"

Watson stared at her for a long moment and then huffed. Evidently, he didn't take either of her threats seriously.

"Suit yourself," she said, setting him on the floor. "I'm just telling you how it will be if you don't quit. You decide what you want to do with the information."

Nose and tail in the air, Watson sauntered across the thick carpet and out the library door.

Faith laughed and began clearing the table. She set the dirty cups and plates as well as the coffeepot and the platter of leftover muffins on a tray. She was about to carry everything to the kitchen when she heard a "psst" from the doorway. She looked up and saw Giselle peeking in.

"All clear?" the young woman asked, glancing around before she came in.

"All clear," Faith assured her. "I'm just tidying up. What can I do for you?"

Giselle held out the library's copy of *Regency Buck*. "I kind of got this one by mistake."

"I thought you might have." Faith smiled as she took the book from her. "Would you like something else?"

"You mentioned Allingham earlier." Giselle went over to the shelves where the historical mysteries were kept. "I wouldn't mind a little Albert Campion."

"Excellent choice," Faith said, showing her the collection. "I think what I admire most about Mrs. Allingham's work is the way her plots are so carefully woven together. Like fine watchworks."

"True." Giselle traced one neatly manicured finger over the titles. "Hmm, should I start with *Mystery Mile* or go right to *The Tiger in the Smoke*? *Tiger*'s my favorite, but *Mystery Mile* is first, and I have a feeling I'm going to be spending a lot of time up in my room reading before the week is over. I might as well begin with the first and read straight through. Well, not *The Crime at Black Dudley*. That's not really a Campion book, even if it was the first one. At least I don't think so."

"I believe Mrs. Allingham hadn't quite decided who she wanted him to be yet." Faith removed *Mystery Mile* and the next four books from the shelf and handed them to Giselle. "These ought to keep you occupied for a while. Though there are many other things to do at the manor besides read. Horseback riding, bicycling, the gym—"

"I know," Giselle interrupted. "I remember all that. I'm sorry, but I just don't want to run into Alex again." She bit her lip.

"He'll be extremely busy with the contest until Friday morning. I doubt you'll see him if you go down to the beach or to the spa or something."

Giselle's mouth tightened, and Faith was afraid even the little she had said about Alex was too much. She was sure of it when Giselle started to cry.

"I'm s-sorry." Giselle tried to blot her face with the back of one hand.

Faith hurried to get her a tissue. "No, *I'm* sorry. I didn't mean to upset you. Is there anything I can do?"

Giselle pressed the tissue to her eyes and then delicately blew her nose. She gave Faith a rueful smile. "Can I talk to you?"

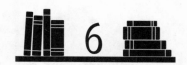

6

Faith shut the library door, then led Giselle to the sofa facing the fireplace.

"Someone might need something, so I can't lock it," Faith said, sitting next to Giselle. "But at least nobody can surprise us."

"I'm sorry," Giselle said again. "I'm not usually this emotional. I know we just met, but if I don't talk to somebody, I think I'm going to explode."

"What about your mother?"

"Good grief, no! Especially not Mother."

"All right," Faith soothed. "I'm not sure if I can be of any help, but I'll be happy to do what I can."

"I don't think there's anything you can do." Giselle sniffled and tucked her legs under her. "Oh, man, I thought I was over this. I really did." She leaned her head back and squeezed her eyes shut. "Why did I have to come on this trip? I told Mother I wanted to stay home, but she wouldn't leave me alone until I agreed to join her."

"I'm sure she meant well."

"I know she did. She couldn't have known Alex would be here. She never even heard his last name. But I should have realized he'd make it to the final round. He told me ages ago that he was going to win this contest."

"You didn't want him to win?" Faith asked.

Giselle flinched. "It's not that. Not exactly. I don't know."

Faith couldn't do much with that and had to settle for looking sympathetic.

Giselle exhaled heavily. "Alex told me he was a writer when we met. He was so ambitious, so determined to get a big contract, and I was sure he'd eventually break through. And he's talented. He really is."

"He must be to have made it this far."

"I assumed Alex wrote military thrillers or legal suspense or something—you know, guy books—and I told him who my mother was. It was a huge surprise to discover he wrote Regency too. After that, he was always asking me questions about Mother—where she came up with her ideas, how she started out, when she got her first contract. It made me wonder if he'd known who I was all along and was only interested in me as a way to get to her."

"Then you had an argument," Faith ventured, certain she knew where this story was headed.

Giselle nodded miserably. "I made all kinds of accusations, and Alex didn't deny them. He simply said that a relationship can't work if there's no trust. That was when he found out he was a finalist in the Central region contest. If he won that contest he'd move to the final round and meet Mother." She blew her nose again, this time not so delicately. "I told him if he loved me, he would drop out. Alex said if I loved him, I wouldn't ask him to make that choice."

"Oh, dear."

"Finally, I told him to leave and not call me again." She swallowed hard and then managed a wobbly grin. "The jerk did exactly what I said I wanted him to do."

"Not even a text?" Faith asked.

Giselle shook her head. "Maybe I should have called him. But Mother said that would be weak and needy."

"Your mother didn't want you to see Alex anymore?"

"Not after I was 'jilted practically at the altar.'" She shrugged. "I guess she wouldn't be much of a writer if she couldn't make even the most mundane situation sound dramatic."

"So you weren't planning to marry him?"

"We'd talked about it a little. Not an actual proposal or anything, just what-ifs." Tears welled up in her eyes. "Now I'm wondering if I should have tried to get him back."

"Is that what you want?"

"Not if he was only using me, like Mother said." Giselle blotted her nose again.

"And if he wasn't?" Faith asked as she handed her the box of tissues.

"If he loved me," Giselle said, helping herself to a handful of tissues, "why didn't he call me or anything?"

"Maybe because you told him not to and he wanted to respect that."

"I know. I know." Giselle sighed. "But Mother says—"

"I'm sure your mother wants the best for you, and it's always a good idea to talk things out with people you love and trust, especially something as important as marriage. But in the end, you're the one who would be marrying Alex, not your mother. Don't you think you should talk this over with him? I mean, if he was lying about his feelings for you to get an in with your mother, she's obviously not going to fall for that at this point. Besides, he has his big opportunity right now. Why would he keep on pretending if he really didn't care for you?"

"After everything I said to him, I wouldn't even know where to begin."

"Apologizing usually helps. And if it doesn't, at least you'll know for sure," Faith said. "Wouldn't that be better than wondering?"

"Maybe." Giselle patted her face with the wad of tissues and then sheepishly dropped it into the trash can beside her. She stood and picked up the stack of Campion books Faith had pulled for her. "Alex doesn't need me bothering him during the contest anyway. I have until Friday to think about whether or not I want to open up old wounds."

"You think about it," Faith said, standing too. "And if you need more books or simply want to talk, you're welcome to come back. I'm here every day."

"Thank you." Giselle hugged the books. "For now, I think these are the best medicine I could have."

Faith gestured to the two levels of books lining the library walls. "We have a whole pharmacy right here whenever you need it."

Giselle smiled, genuinely this time. "Thanks for talking to me. I'll see you around."

Faith watched her leave, wishing she knew something more to tell her. What she had said was sound advice, but Faith understood it was hard to be certain about anyone. She had met a man she thought she'd live happily ever after with, and he had deceived her with someone else. What if Alex was like John?

But what if he wasn't? If Alex and Giselle were right for each other, if they were truly in love, it would be a shame for them to lose out on a great life together just because Giselle was afraid. And how much of that fear had she gotten from her mother?

Faith imagined it must be hard for rich and famous people to weed out sincere friends from the hangers-on, from those who thought they could profit from any kind of relationship. In many ways, it was a blessing to not have too much money. Then again, she hadn't been rich, but John had still betrayed her. Some people apparently didn't need the financial motivation.

She shook her head. She wasn't going to let an unpleasant memory spoil her day. Still, she was glad the Candle House Book Club had a meeting scheduled for tonight. She didn't want to stay home alone.

"Oh, it sounds delicious." Brooke clasped her hands together, blue eyes sparkling as she plopped herself down into a cozy chair in front of the Candle House Library's unlit fireplace. "It's love at first sight."

Faith laughed, reaching down to pet Watson who was sitting at her feet. "Melanie and Tony hardly know each other."

"That's what makes it so romantic," Brooke reasoned. "Besides, I've seen him. Who wouldn't be interested?"

"Okay, Melanie's definitely interested, but she doesn't have time for romance right now. Not with the contest going on."

"You ought to run him by Diva and Bling," Eileen Piper said, a touch of humor in her gently lined face. Faith's aunt—a fellow librarian and the leader of the book club—was always amused by Brooke's reliance on her angelfish to reveal the trustworthiness of any man. "Just to be sure."

"You're right," Brooke said thoughtfully. "If I didn't think it would upset their tummies if I carried them over to the manor, I definitely would. Maybe I could talk to Tony over the phone for a few minutes."

"It's probably best if you don't upset your pets." Midge Foster, the local vet and owner of Happy Tails Gourmet Bakery, smiled at the napping Chihuahua curled up on her lap. Atticus was a fixture at all the book club meetings. "I'm sure Melanie and Tony can figure things out for themselves if they want to."

"Still, wouldn't it be great if they eloped?" Brooke said.

"By the end of the week?" Eileen laughed. "Probably not a good idea outside of one of Camilla Courtenay's books. And then at least one of them would need a title of some kind and a vast fortune."

"And one of them would be running away from an unwanted match," Midge added.

Faith shook her head. "I don't suppose that happens much anymore."

"Sometimes," Brooke said wisely. "Haven't you heard about the baronet from England who ran away from his aunt, the Duchess of Farrellsmoor, so he wouldn't have to marry the deadly Lady Phillipa Lambton?"

Midge rolled her eyes. "I doubt it was like that."

"Anyway, he disappeared somewhere and won't come back, and Lady Phillipa's parents had to announce that the marriage would not take place. It raised more than a few eyebrows, even though everyone said it was a mutual decision."

"It probably was a mutual decision," Eileen said, "no matter what some scandal sheet says."

"It wasn't a scandal sheet," Brooke insisted. "It was a blog."

"Oh, well, that makes all the difference." Eileen glanced slyly at Faith. Brooke huffed and didn't say anything else.

"Whatever the reason for the breakup," Midge said, "Lord Whoever was probably smart to end an engagement with someone he didn't love. And somewhere along the road I'm sure he'll find someone who does suit him."

"Men like that always find someone if they want to," Eileen said.

"It's not always so easy," Faith said. "Even when you think you have it all worked out, things can change. And maybe the right one isn't out there at all."

Watson jumped onto Faith's lap and looked at her with what she perceived as concern.

"Of course he is." Aunt Eileen squeezed Faith's hand. "Who wouldn't want a wonderful woman like you?"

"Evidently a lot of guys." Faith managed a smile as she scratched behind Watson's ears. "But better no one than the wrong one, don't you think?"

"I know that's right. I could tell you stories all night. Good thing Diva and Bling let me know when I've got a loser on my hands. But that doesn't mean I'm not still looking, and you should be too. And maybe," Brooke said, trading smirks with Eileen and Midge, "you won't have to look very far."

Faith knew she was blushing, even though Brooke frequently teased her about the handsome owner of Castleton Manor. Wolfe was her boss and nothing more. It would be foolish to expect anything else. "Let's be realistic here. I'm not twenty-five anymore."

"You're not eighty either," Eileen said firmly. "I promise you that thirty-nine isn't the end of the world. You're just too discerning to bother with men who aren't good enough for you."

"That's what I keep telling myself."

"And you're better off without that creep you were seeing before you moved here," Brooke added.

"Now *that*," Faith said, "I'm sure of."

"All right now," Eileen broke in, "since this is supposed to be a book club, we ought to discuss this month's book. Who would like to begin?"

"Oooh, me!" Brooke said. "Me!"

Eileen smiled at her. "Go ahead."

"I thought it was wonderful," Brooke said breathlessly. "I mean, it didn't have any racy parts, but it was *so* romantic. When the duke told his wife that she had been the right bride for him all along, I thought I was going to cry."

"I loved that part," Midge said. "After all Venetia had done to catch him—and I was surprised how underhanded she was sometimes—Branton forgave her and assured her that he loved her anyway." She gave a happy sigh.

"I'm glad nobody's forced to get married these days simply because he caught a woman he thought was fainting," Faith remarked. "I don't know that I'd want to end up with anyone I had to trick into marriage."

"I think Venetia was lucky that Branton was a good man and didn't hold any of her antics against her. When she told . . ." Eileen frowned. "I can't remember the name of the viscount who was her uncle, and I don't know where my copy of the book disappeared to."

"I'm sure yours will turn up." Faith made her expression blandly innocent as she handed Eileen her own copy of Camilla Courtenay's *A Love Abandoned*. "For now, you can use mine."

Eileen flipped through the pages until she found what she wanted. "Chevalier. I don't know why, but no matter how many times I've read that one, I always want to say Chauvelin. Anyway, he was the one who made her do all those things to catch Branton and then turned on her when she refused to give him any more of her husband's money."

"I was afraid Branton was going to cast Venetia off when Chevalier told him lies about her and forged those awful letters," Brooke said.

"And so was she." Midge grinned. "Personally, I was glad when her uncle had to flee to the Continent in disgrace once Branton stood by his wife and discredited him."

"It's nice they had their happily ever after," Faith said. "Though I don't know how many men could forgive that quickly and easily, especially when having to marry Venetia forced him to give up Louisa Carlisle, the woman he had wanted to offer to."

"But Venetia loved him much more than Louisa ever would have," Brooke said passionately. "He realized that in the end. And he loved her too."

"After all," Eileen said, a glint of humor in her eyes, "it *is* fiction."

As Faith drove back to her cottage that night with Watson riding in his favorite spot in the passenger seat, she wondered about Camilla and Ann Giordano. Ann had said that the past was too heavy a burden to carry for long. But had she forgiven whatever had been between her and Camilla?

Branton had forgiven Venetia unreservedly, but did that ever really happen outside the pages of a novel?

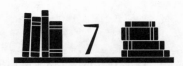

The next morning when Faith entered the manor with Watson, the cat immediately veered toward the stairs. No doubt he was headed to the second floor to search for the Pomeranian.

Faith wasn't surprised to find one of the contestants waiting for her to open the library, but for some reason she *was* surprised to see it was Ann.

"Good morning," Faith said, walking a little faster as she crossed the gallery. "I hope you haven't been waiting long."

"Just all night," Ann said good-humoredly. "I'm not much of a technology person, but I do miss having access to the Internet when I'm working, especially when it's about two in the morning and the library is closed."

"I suppose that would slow you down." Faith unlocked the door and ushered her inside. "Now what can I help you with? I see you have a list."

Ann nodded and consulted the piece of paper she held. "I need something on the traditional meanings of different flowers. I want to know the time it took to sail to China from England and back again in 1817. And . . ." She looked around to make sure no one was coming into the library. "I need to find out if there were circumstances where a nobleman's baseborn child could claim his inheritance."

"I don't think so. At least not his title and any entailed property. Otherwise, the man could leave his estate to anyone he chose simply by putting it into his will."

"I was afraid that might be the case." Ann shrugged. "I guess I'll have to figure out some other kind of complication."

"I can do an Internet search for you in case I'm not remembering correctly," Faith offered. "I'm afraid the most helpful book we have on nineteenth-century inheritance law has been loaned out. I can let you know when it's available again."

Ann tilted her head to one side, a knowing gleam in her dark eyes. "Camilla has it, doesn't she? No, you don't have to tell me. It's exactly the sort of book she'd need to plot out her next novel. She almost always has some kind of legal mix-up in her stories."

"You seem familiar with her books."

"You could say I've followed her career with interest," Ann replied.

"I suppose the two of you know each other very well."

"We used to. At least I thought we did." There was something almost wistful in Ann's expression. "That was twenty-five years ago, and I was wrong then too. I haven't seen her since. Not before last night. You probably wouldn't guess that we used to be best friends."

Faith raised her eyebrows, but she didn't interrupt.

"We once shared an apartment in New York City when both of us were struggling to make it as writers. I was a bookkeeper in a company that made typewriters, and she was a waitress in an upscale restaurant that was popular with the executive types. Back then she was a cute little slip of a thing who earned a lot of tips, and we managed to scrape by together. We'd read each other's work, catch typos, and give feedback, but we never got that much done. It seemed like there was always something in the real world that needed to be taken care of."

"That's understandable."

Ann smiled. "Don't get me wrong. It wasn't all work all the time. We had fun. Then I got serious about a man I was dating." Her smile stiffened. "I'm sure you can already tell where this is going."

Faith winced slightly. "She took your boyfriend."

"That pretty much sums it up, but it's much more convoluted than that. Sterling had been seeing Camilla before he and I met. I thought it was over between them, or I never would have gone out with him in the first place. We dated for a few months, and it was going so well I was sure we'd get married before long. Then out of the blue he and Camilla ran off together. He said he was sorry, but that was the only explanation I ever got, and it was the last time I saw either of them."

"Wait a minute. Sterling? Sterling Courtenay? You were going to marry Sterling Courtenay?"

Ann chuckled. "Don't act so surprised. I wasn't too bad looking myself when I was young."

"No, it's not that at all. But I assumed Camilla must have met him after she had some success with her books. I mean, wasn't he some kind of financier or something? He must have had money."

"Yes, he did. But they met at the restaurant. Sterling was a regular customer of Camilla's."

"How did you meet him?"

"Camilla invited me to have dinner at the restaurant as a treat for my birthday, and she introduced us. We hit it off right away, and then suddenly it was over." Ann shrugged, but it was obvious that the memory still brought her pain. "The worst part is that it wasn't like him. I didn't think he was the kind of guy who'd say he loved you and then dump you the next day. But I was wrong about him too."

Faith couldn't think of a thing to say.

"Anyway, that's all in the past. He died five years ago. And if he loved Camilla enough to stay with her for the rest of his life, I guess it's better that he married her and not me. I just want to make sure that what happened between me and Camilla doesn't affect the way my contest entry is judged."

"I wouldn't think she'd have anything against you," Faith said. "More like the other way around."

"I've got too many things to do with my life. Carrying around an old grudge isn't anywhere near the top of my list." Ann smiled. "Winning this contest is."

"Why don't you have a seat? I'll get you that book on the meaning of flowers, and then I'll see what I can find on the Internet about ship travel to China and Regency inheritance laws. How would that be?"

"Very helpful." There was a softness in Ann's expression that hadn't been there before. "And thanks for listening. The only person I ever told about Sterling and Camilla was my mother, and she passed away eleven years ago. It was good to talk it out again. Besides, why would I want to marry someone who wanted someone else?"

Faith laughed softly. "I know I wouldn't want to do it."

Faith half-expected Melanie Wilde to make her way down to the library sometime that day and confide some secret heartache of her own, but she never did. She concluded with a grin that Melanie simply wasn't the confiding type and that she might not be burdened with a secret heartache anyway. It seemed a little too soon for her to be pining over Tony, no matter what Brooke said.

Faith was walking across the gallery when she saw Watson lounging at the bottom of the stairs. "Come on, Rumpy. It's time to go home."

He glanced at her and then looked pointedly away.

"Aren't you hungry?"

He got to his feet, but rather than coming to her, he padded up the stairs.

"Watson." She headed toward him.

But that only made him pick up speed. It was no use trying to catch him if he didn't want to be caught.

"Fine. I'm going home to get ready for my dinner. I may or may not put out anything for you."

Watson stared down at her from his lofty perch at the top of the stairs, then disappeared into the hallway.

Faith dressed a little more casually for dinner that night. Ralph had invited her to join him and Camilla and the three finalists to discuss the progress they were making and, as he said, to make sure they all took a break and had a decent meal at least once a day.

When Faith entered the banquet hall, she was surprised to see that not only Tony and Jenny were present, along with Ralph and Camilla, but Giselle was too. None of the contestants had arrived yet.

Once she had greeted everyone, Faith sat down next to Giselle. "Are you sure you want to be here tonight?" she whispered.

Giselle shrugged. "Alex and I didn't exactly get along very well earlier. I thought that I could try to normalize things between us. I can start out being civil and see what happens. I mean, if he can't even stand to be at the same table as me, it probably won't do any good for me to try to talk to him, right?"

"Maybe not," Faith said, and then she turned to Camilla when she noticed her looking quizzically at them. "Did you and Emma have a good time today?"

"We did, didn't we, sugar?" Camilla cooed.

Emma yipped from the chair at Camilla's right.

"We played on the beach, and we both had a nice massage. Jenny got Emma a strawberry pupcake from the bakery. Giselle, you should have come with us."

Giselle squirmed a little. "I was reading."

"Maybe next time then." Camilla smiled at her daughter. "I'm glad you decided to have dinner with us. We'll try not to talk business all night, I promise."

"No," Ralph said. "I want everybody to relax, at least during the meal. We'll get a quick update from everybody, make sure no one needs anything for now, and that'll be it for shoptalk. More importantly, we want to get to know the finalists better so we can see how they'll fit in at Northanger. And, Faith, maybe you can tell everyone about the ball."

"I'll be happy to," Faith said. "I'm really looking forward to it. It'll be fun to dress up."

"Are we talking about Friday night?" Melanie asked as she and her fellow contestants walked into the room. She glanced at Tony when she sat down, then smiled at Ralph. "I have the most amazing dress. It would be great for a cover shoot. I'd be happy to let Northanger borrow it. You'll have to look at it and let me know what you think."

"That might be interesting," Ralph said, though he didn't seem as excited about the idea as Melanie was. "Remind me about that on Friday, Tony."

"I'll certainly do that. I'm sure it will be a lovely sight." Tony bowed his head in Melanie's direction.

Faith noticed a touch of pink on Melanie's cheeks.

"What about you, Ann?" Camilla asked, a slight hopefulness in her voice as she addressed her old friend.

"I'm not sure how amazing it will be, but I have something that will do. I don't know any country dances or anything like that, but I can waltz."

"You've got me there," Alex said. "I don't do any of that. Someone tried to teach me once, but we never really got very far."

Giselle blinked as if something was in her eye, then stared down at her empty plate.

"I'm sure it's not too late," Faith offered. "Just a matter of taking the time to learn."

"Time," Alex said coolly, "is something I don't have." He didn't say anything more as the Caesar chiffonade was served.

Camilla made much of the shrimp and Parmesan cheese nestled in fresh romaine lettuce as the dressing was passed around the table.

"Everything is so delicious," she said, dousing her salad when her daughter passed her the sauceboat. "I tell you what, Emmie. We are definitely coming back here when we have a chance."

The little dog panted at her and eagerly accepted a piece of shrimp.

"As I was telling everyone," Ralph said when the rest of the party began to eat, "we're not going to spend much time on business tonight. I'm sure you three have been working very hard on your entries and need a break, so we'll keep this brief. I'd like to hear how each of you is doing getting your story down. Melanie?"

"It's coming along," she said with a smile. "I'm working on my chapter first, and then I'll see where that takes me as far as my plot."

Alex shook his head. "I could never do that. I'm working on my plot. If I don't know where I'm headed from the beginning, I waste too much time wandering around trying to find my story."

"But that takes all the fun out of it," Melanie retorted. "If I already knew what happened, I'd be too bored with the story to ever write it."

Ralph chuckled. "I promise you, Northanger Press never tells any of its authors *how* to go about writing their books. Whatever works for you works for us."

"That's one thing whoever wins is going to love." Camilla took a large bite of her salad, swallowed, and then dabbed her mouth with her napkin. "Ralph never interferes. He doesn't do anything but make my books better."

"Only because I have such great material to work with in the first place," Ralph responded. "Now how about you, Ann? Are you making progress?"

Ann nodded. "So far, so good."

"Do you plan everything out or just wing it?"

"I suppose I do a little of both. I know where I want to begin and where I want to end and a few major stops along the way, but after that I go along to see what happens."

Camilla took another bite, nodding eagerly. "That's exactly what

I do. It keeps me from wandering too much, but it leaves me free to explore too. When I was working on *Lady at the Hazard*—oh, what is it now? Twenty years ago? Anyway, I knew from the start that I wanted Charlotte to meet—" She stopped and cleared her throat. "I wanted her to meet—" She licked her lips, then took a sip of water.

"Are you all right?" Faith asked.

Everyone at the table was looking at Camilla now.

"Camilla?" Ralph said, standing up.

Camilla was wheezing faintly, and her lips were definitely swollen. "Jenny," she gasped. "M-my purse."

Emma stood up on her cushion and barked while Jenny dug through Camilla's purse, taking out and discarding three or four bottles before selecting one. She wrenched it open and shook out two pills into Camilla's trembling hand.

Camilla popped the pills into her mouth and swallowed half a glass of water, collapsing into her chair afterward, clinging to the arms, her breath still coming in ragged gasps.

Giselle looked desperately at her mother. "Are you all right? Do you need anything? What do you want me to do?" She glared at the dog. "Emma, be quiet!"

The little dog barked one last time before settling down, her button eyes fixed on Camilla.

Still gasping, Camilla waved one hand. "Wait . . . a minute. I don't . . . think it's that bad."

"What's the matter?" Ralph pressed. "What happened?"

Giselle whirled around. "Were there peanuts in the salad?" she asked Faith. "Even little pieces? Mother's extremely allergic."

"I know she is," Faith said calmly. "The executive chef and all the kitchen staff were made aware. They were very careful to avoid using anything with peanut or peanut oil in it." She turned to Camilla. "Do you want to go to the emergency room?"

"No," Camilla wheezed. "I think it's getting better." Her hands shook as she drank a little more water, and then she took a few hitching breaths. Emma wriggled her way onto Camilla's lap, and Camilla held her close, squeezing her eyes shut for a long moment.

"I don't think it's too bad," Jenny said as she refilled Camilla's water glass. "We've dealt with this before, and usually the Benadryl does the trick. We haven't had to use the EpiPen so far, but it's a good thing we have one. Just in case."

"Is there anything I can do?" Alex asked Giselle.

She shook her head.

Camilla rubbed her mouth. "Itches."

"Are you sure you shouldn't go to the emergency room?" Faith asked, though Camilla did seem to be breathing easier now.

Camilla managed a bit of a smile. "I don't think so. Last time I went, it took them so long to get to me that I was completely back to normal by then. If I had really had a problem, I guess I would have gone ahead and died."

"Mother," Giselle said, "it wasn't as bad as that."

"Well, it might have been," Camilla said, with a touch of mischief in her expression. "It was scary enough." Her breathing was still labored, but she didn't seem to be in as much distress as before. "I think, though, that Emma and I ought to go lie down for a while."

Jenny stood immediately, scooping up Camilla's purse and her dog.

"Do you want me to come with you?" Giselle asked.

"No, don't do that." Camilla paused, trying to catch a deeper breath and not quite succeeding. "It's been hard enough to get you out of your room. This is nothing serious, and I don't want to spoil everyone's dinner." She shook her head. "I just can't imagine what I could have gotten ahold of to give me a reaction like that."

"Is there anything else you're allergic to besides peanuts?" Faith asked.

"Peanuts are the worst, but I have a few other allergies, mostly to pollen and other things floating around in the air. But none of that affects me like peanuts."

Giselle took her arm. "Are you really all right?"

"I'm fine, honey." Camilla freed herself with a motherly pat. "You stay down here and enjoy your dinner. All of you, please. Don't let my allergies put a damper on things. You don't actually need me, do you, Ralph?"

"We'll be fine. You rest and get better."

"Are you certain she shouldn't be going to hospital?" Tony asked. Then he glanced at Faith and cleared his throat. "It would be better if she went to the hospital, wouldn't it? Just to be sure nothing's seriously wrong."

Ralph shook one finger at Jenny. "If she's not better soon, you let me know. Something like this shouldn't be taken lightly."

Jenny nodded and led Camilla out of the banquet hall.

Alex stood and looked at Giselle with concern, but when she gave him a slight smile, he abruptly sat down again. "I guess there's no reason we shouldn't finish dinner," he said. "As long as Camilla's okay and everything."

There was a faint air of wariness as they all finished their salads, but it was gone by the time the baked salmon roulade, snow peas and carrots julienne, and red potatoes arrived. By then Melanie was giggling over Tony's description of the literature professor he'd had in college, and Ann and Ralph were discussing the impact of independent publishing on traditional houses.

When everyone had finished the tiramisu and coffee, Giselle gave up her hesitant attempts to make small talk with Alex and got up from the table. "I'm going to check on my mother. She's had these incidents before, so I suppose she'll be fine, but I'd better go see." She turned to Faith. "Are you sure there couldn't have been anything related to peanuts in the food? Accidentally, I mean."

"I'll double-check, but I don't think so. Our staff had explicit instructions about that before any of you arrived."

That look of concern was back on Alex's face, but now it was touched with regret. Perhaps he was sorry for being so cool toward Giselle. "You don't think Camilla would have eaten those peanuts we had in our rooms, do you? Surely she would have known better if she's that allergic."

"Of course she would," Giselle said firmly. "She's really careful about it."

"In your room?" Faith asked. "What do you mean?"

"We had—" Alex glanced at Ann and Melanie. "At least *I* had a packet of peanuts in my room. It was with the fruit bowl and the box of chocolates. I assumed everyone got some."

Faith frowned. "The manor never puts peanuts in the rooms."

"I had fruit and chocolates," Ralph said. "I assumed they were in all the suites."

"They are," Faith told him. "They're put in each room before the guests check in but not peanuts. We don't do peanuts." She didn't say it aloud, but she knew Marlene would object to anything so pedestrian at Castleton Manor. "Did any of the rest of you get peanuts?"

"I did," Melanie said.

Tony nodded.

"I did too," Ann said. "I ate them last night while I was working on my plot."

Faith frowned. "I'll check with our assistant manager and with the kitchen, but I don't think the peanuts came from us."

"To be honest," Melanie said, "I thought it was a little odd. The fruit was nice and the chocolates were gourmet, but those peanuts were—well, cheap. I'm not complaining or anything, but they looked like something you'd pick up in the airport, not the type of thing a place like this would put in their guests' rooms."

"We'll have to ask Camilla if she had peanuts in her room too," Ralph said.

"But if they were in her room," Faith said, "she knew not to eat them or even touch them. And if she had, she would have reacted then, not at the dinner table. If she ate them right before she came downstairs, she would have known before dinner was served. Those kinds of reactions take just a few minutes. The peanuts must have been in something she ate at dinner tonight, and she only had the salad."

"There weren't any nuts in the salad," Giselle said. "At least, not in mine."

"Not in anyone's," Faith replied. "The kitchen wouldn't put them in that sort of salad, even if they hadn't been warned about her allergy ahead of time. And the peanuts would have been obvious if they had been in there." She thought for a minute. "The only thing it could have been in was the dressing."

"Would your chef put peanut oil in the dressing for a Caesar chiffonade?" Tony asked.

Faith gave him a puzzled look.

Tony smiled. "I'm a bit of a dabbler in the kitchen, and that's one of my favorite salads."

"I don't think that's part of the chef's recipe," Faith said. "There's only olive oil with Dijon mustard, lemon juice, and garlic. I've made it myself before. I've never heard of anyone putting peanut oil in it."

"There was something else in it," Ann said, narrowing her eyes. "I don't exactly know what it was, but I could taste something more. It could have been peanut."

Faith hadn't paid that much attention to the dressing. Had it tasted different? She glanced at the table. It was littered with dessert plates and coffee cups, dirty forks and spoons, a nearly empty coffeepot, a sugar bowl, and a half-full container of creamer. But everything else, including the sauceboat with the salad dressing in it, had been cleared away long before.

Knowing how the kitchen at the manor was run, she was sure everything had already been rinsed and put in the dishwasher. But whether or not it could be proven now, it seemed clear that the only way Camilla could have come into contact with peanuts was in the salad dressing.

"I'll check with the kitchen one more time," Faith told everyone. "In case someone didn't get the message. We don't want any more accidents happening."

Marlene was in the kitchen when Faith went down to talk to Brooke.

"I heard about the incident at dinner," Marlene said to Faith. "How bad was it?"

Brooke looked worriedly at Faith. Obviously, she had already been raked over the coals.

"It could have been serious," Faith admitted, "but it wasn't. Camilla knows how bad her peanut allergy is and was prepared to handle it. She didn't even have to use her EpiPen."

Marlene pursed her thin lips. "I carefully explained her allergy to both of you. How could this have happened? Can you imagine how it could have affected the manor if Camilla had died?"

"It would have been hard on Camilla as well," Faith murmured.

Marlene glared at her. "This could have been a tragedy. There's nothing amusing about it."

"Not at all."

"I'm sorry it happened," Brooke said, "but I promise you there was no peanut oil in anything we served this evening."

"As far as I can tell, there wasn't anything it could have been in besides the salad dressing," Faith said. "Camilla was fine when she came to the table, and she didn't have a chance to eat anything but the salad. Is there any possibility that one of your assistants could have used peanut oil without thinking? Maybe someone hadn't heard about Camilla yet."

Brooke shook her head. "For one thing, I told everyone in the kitchen about her allergy. I made it very, very clear that as long as Camilla was here, there wasn't to be peanut anything even near the kitchen."

"And the other thing?" Marlene said primly.

"I made that dressing myself. I know exactly what went into it, and none of it was peanuts or peanut oil. There was nothing related to nuts in the entire meal."

Marlene studied Brooke for a moment. "You have a word with your staff. Ensure they all know not to make any mistakes like this again. Don't force me to speak to them myself."

Brooke nodded.

"I still think Ms. Courtenay should go to the hospital. If she has some kind of secondary reaction, I don't know what our liability would be. I'm going to see if I can at least persuade a doctor to come out and examine her." With that Marlene left the kitchen, the sharp taps of her heels on the floor eventually fading into silence.

Brooke exhaled heavily and dropped into a nearby chair.

"I know you wouldn't make a mistake like that." Faith sat down beside her. "And don't worry. Camilla is perfectly fine."

"Marlene is right. It could have been a tragedy."

"But it wasn't, okay?"

Brooke nodded.

"It is strange, though," Faith said. "There's no reason there should have been peanut oil in that dressing. So the real question is, who put it in there and why? If it wasn't done in the kitchen, it must have been done either on the way from the kitchen to the table or at the table."

"It wasn't in the kitchen. The dressing was the last thing I did before the salads went out. They were literally on the tray when I set the sauceboat on there. Myself."

"All right, that rules out the kitchen. What about from the kitchen to the table?"

Brooke shrugged. "I don't know why any of the kitchen staff would put peanut oil in the dressing on the way to the banquet hall. It doesn't make sense."

"No, it doesn't. And they wouldn't have run into anyone on their way up. Everyone who's connected to the contest was already at the table before the salads were brought in. That leaves only the people at the table."

Brooke frowned. "Wouldn't at least one person notice someone pouring something into the dressing as it was being passed around?"

"Maybe. Maybe not. People were talking, passing not only the sauceboat but butter and rolls, salt and pepper, sugar and cream. You know how it is. Someone could have had a little vial of oil in a napkin or in the palm of the hand. Camilla is so allergic that it wouldn't have taken much." Faith stopped for a moment to consider. "Or it could have been ground-up peanuts. If they were crushed very fine, no one would have noticed. The pieces would have looked like seasoning. What do you think?"

"It's possible." Brooke appeared troubled. "But that would mean—"

"Someone meant to do it," Faith said quietly. "It was deliberate."

The two of them stared at each other. It was hardly believable, but what other explanation was there?

"But why?" Brooke said. "Do you think it was supposed to be a joke?"

"Not exactly a funny one, if you ask me."

"Could somebody want to keep Camilla from judging the contest?" Brooke asked.

"I don't know why. The three finalists wouldn't want anything standing in the way of them getting their big chance. It might never come around again."

"I thought you said Camilla had some history with one of them."

"Ann," Faith said. "But she claims that's old news and all she wants is a fair shake in the contest. At this point I don't have any reason not to believe her."

"I suppose not." Brooke's forehead wrinkled. "Okay, if it was someone at the table and we rule out the three contestants, who else could it have been?"

Faith recalled who was sitting where at the table. "Emma was in the chair next to Camilla, and Jenny was next to the dog. Ralph was at one end of the table with Tony on his right. Melanie, Ann, and Alex were next to Tony. And Giselle sat between me and her mother. That's all."

Brooke appeared pensive for a moment and then managed a slight smile. "I'm sure it wasn't Emma."

Faith smiled too. "Camilla is fine. Whatever happened, it didn't end up being serious, and it definitely wasn't your fault. Try not to worry."

"I'll try."

Faith glanced around the immaculate kitchen. "It looks like you're done for the night." She stood and pulled her friend to her feet. "Why don't you go home and get a good night's sleep? I'm going to check on Camilla and see what else I can find out."

"Why do you always have to be that way?"

Faith had been about to knock on Camilla's door, but she stopped herself and dropped her raised hand. It was Giselle's voice, and the young woman didn't sound happy. Not wanting to intrude, Faith began to turn around and walk away.

The door flew open, and Giselle jumped back, obviously startled to see Faith. "I . . . didn't know anyone was out here."

"I wanted to see if your mother was doing better."

Giselle stepped out into the corridor and shut the door behind her.

"Is everything okay?" Faith asked.

Giselle's lips quivered. "I told her about Alex and me."

"You did? Why?"

"She wanted to know why Alex was acting the way he was at dinner. She always notices stuff like that. And stupid me—" Giselle's voice broke, and she waved one hand in front of her tear-filled eyes. "I couldn't help crying when she asked me about it. He's going to hate me even more than he already does when he finds out I've spoiled his chance to get a book contract."

"I don't see how that could be," Faith soothed, handing her a tissue from her purse. "The entries will be anonymous. Your mother hasn't seen anyone's writing so far. How could she possibly know which one is Alex's?"

Giselle shrugged.

"I think you're worrying about something that will never happen." Faith glanced toward Camilla's door. "Do you think she's up to having a visitor for a few minutes?"

"Oh, sure. She's all right now." Giselle pushed the door open again, not bothering to knock. "Is it okay if Faith comes in?"

"Please do," Camilla called.

Giselle waved Faith inside, then shut the door after her.

"Emma and I are delighted that you've come calling." Camilla was reclining in the heavily draped bed, surrounded by oversize down pillows. She wore a mauve bed jacket. Emma, sitting on a cushion next to her, had a matching mauve ribbon on top of her head.

"It's my pleasure," Faith said. "How are you feeling?"

"I told everyone it was nothing. Ms. Russell insisted I have a doctor come see me, but I said that was the last thing I needed if I was going to start feeling better."

"I'm sure she was worried about you," Faith said, pulling up one of the ornate chairs next to the bed and taking a seat. "We all were."

"I wish I knew what could have caused that reaction in the first place." Camilla seemed more confused than upset. "I'm always so careful."

"I talked to the sous-chef about it. She made the dressing personally, and she's sure there wasn't anything related to peanuts in it."

"Maybe I've developed a new allergy. My doctor says that happens sometimes." Camilla sighed. "I don't want to go through all those tests again. They're unpleasant, and I have so much to do."

Faith studied her for a moment, not sure how much she ought to say, but if something was going on, it would be better to find out sooner rather than later. "Do you think someone could have deliberately put something in the salad dressing? It seems pretty obvious that was the only thing you had that could have been tampered with."

Camilla's blue eyes widened, and then she shrugged. "Don't be silly. Who in the world would do something like that? It's got to be no more than a careless mistake. Maybe someone in the kitchen put something wrong in the recipe. Or like I said, maybe I've developed a new allergy."

"And what about the lamp?"

Camilla frowned. "The lamp? What does that have to do with anything?"

"I'm not sure," Faith admitted. "I'm just wondering. You said it was on your bathroom counter."

"Right. It was one of those little Tiffany lamps, something to give the room some ambience."

"It just shorted out when you turned it on?"

"Yes. That night before dinner I went into the bathroom to look in the mirror, and I turned on the lamp. I had no sooner switched it on when it shorted out. Housekeeping brought me something else, but I didn't want that big, bulky thing they showed up with. I told the man that I'd wait until the first one could be fixed."

"I don't want to worry you unnecessarily," Faith said, "but have you thought about what might have happened if you had been in the bathtub when you switched on that lamp?"

Camilla pulled her little dog closer to her on the bed. "What are you saying?"

"I'm not saying anything yet. I'm only asking questions. You've had two incidents since you got here. Neither one of them ended up being very serious, but each of them could have been fatal. Don't you think that's strange?"

Camilla bit her lip and didn't reply at first. "I think it's a little ridiculous to take a couple of accidents and try to make them into some murder plot." She smiled abruptly. "It's very kind of you to be concerned about me, but I promise it's unnecessary. Who could possibly want to kill me?"

"Was there anyone at dinner who you think might do something like that?" Faith pressed.

"Of course not," Camilla protested. "I'm sure none of them would do anything to hurt me or anyone else, and I've never even met the three finalists before."

"What about Ann?"

"Well, I used to know Ann, but that was a long time ago, and my husband is dead. There's nothing left for us to squabble over, right?" She patted Faith's arm. "I know how it is, honey. You're like me. You can't help but see a story in everything. But sometimes real life isn't all that exciting or dramatic. That's why we need good books."

9

The next morning, Faith got dressed quickly. She rushed out the door and over to the manor with Watson at her heels. As soon as they entered, Watson scampered away.

"Don't get into any trouble," she called after him.

Faith was crossing the lobby when she saw Wolfe walking toward her.

"Good morning," he said, his smile as engaging as ever. "You're out and about early, aren't you?"

"You are too. Anything special going on?"

"I was just coming to talk to Marlene. She said there was an incident last night, but she didn't give any details in her message, and I got in too late to call her back. Do you know what she's talking about?"

Faith filled him in on Camilla's allergic reaction at dinner. "I talked to Camilla last night. She really is fine, and she doesn't seem too upset by what happened. But I wish I could figure out how peanut oil could have gotten into the salad dressing. It doesn't make sense."

"Maybe I should talk to Brooke about it."

"I already did," Faith told him. "She made that dressing herself. No peanut oil. No peanut products in the kitchen at all."

Wolfe narrowed his eyes. "What aren't you telling me?"

She felt her face heat slightly. "It's not something I'm keeping from you, though I didn't realize I was being so obvious."

He chuckled.

"I don't actually have any evidence at the moment," Faith hedged.

"But you're wondering if someone might have deliberately done something to Camilla."

She raised her eyebrows. "You don't sound surprised."

"Not after what Camilla said about the lamp in her bathroom

shorting out. I realize things like that happen, especially with antiques, but it was still pretty shocking—" There was sudden amusement in his blue eyes. "Sorry. No pun intended."

Faith fought a smile.

"Anyway, it surprised me to hear about that lamp. Mack's not the type to let anything like that get past him."

"I was thinking the same thing. I came in a little early so I could ask if he'd examined the lamp. He ought to know if it has been tampered with."

Faith and Wolfe made their way down to the basement, past the kitchen and the laundry, and into the workroom. It was filled with shelves and tables, all crammed with a baffling assortment of old machinery, a collection of power tools, and other odds and ends. A stoop-shouldered old man with a full head of bushy white hair was leaning over a well-worn notebook, scribbling away. Faith could see columns of numbers on the page before him.

Wolfe knocked on the open door. "Mack?"

The old man started and then turned. "Mr. Jaxon. Miss Newberry. Good morning."

"Still won't use a calculator?" Wolfe teased.

Mack had been at Castleton Manor longer than anyone else save for Wolfe's mother, and Faith got the impression that, even grown up, Wolfe was rather in awe of the man. And very fond of him too.

Mack shook his head. "I'd rather use what brains I have as long as I have 'em. I don't want to be like some people who can't make change for a dollar without pulling out some kind of gadget."

"Are you planning something out?" Faith asked. Since she had been at the manor, she had come to appreciate Mack's ability to repair anything from plumbing and lighting to appliances and even vehicles, as well as his capacity to build and repair nearly anything made out of wood.

"Yes. The wind blew down one of the fences out by the stables, and I was calculating how much wood I'd need to put up a new one."

"You can't fix the old one?" Wolfe asked.

"I could fix it, but it's that old one at the back of the paddock that's already come down twice before. If it's all the same to you, I'd just as soon build a new one as keep propping up the old." Mack sighed. "Those four-legged devils out there know it's pretty well worn-out, and from what I can see of it, they keep trying it. One day they'll push the whole thing over themselves, and we'll have a time trying to get 'em all back. Might be it wasn't the wind that knocked it down this time."

Faith hid a smile, knowing Mack loved the manor's horses every bit as much as he loved his circular saw and nail gun.

"I'll leave that for you to decide. You're the expert," Wolfe told him. "Faith and I came to ask you about something else."

"Yes sir?"

"I understand one of the lamps shorted out a few days ago. I suppose somebody brought it down to you."

The old man nodded, jerking his thumb toward a shelf in the back corner. "That one over there. I haven't looked at it yet with everything else I got to do. I sent up another lamp from storage, but I guess her ladyship didn't care for it and sent it back."

"Marlene?" Wolfe asked.

"Oh no," Mack said. "Not Ms. Russell. Not this time."

"I think it was Camilla who didn't approve of the new one," Faith explained.

"None of 'em are new," Mack grumbled. "But they were all in tip-top condition. I can promise you that, Mr. Jaxon."

"I trust they were. Would you mind taking a look at it now?" Wolfe asked. "I'm not saying you need to work on it right away, but maybe you can give us an idea of what's wrong with it."

"Sure thing." Mack shuffled over to the shelf, picked up the small lamp, and brought it back to his worktable. He removed the stained glass shade to reveal the blackened light bulb that he twisted out and set on the table. Next he took off the brass sleeve where the bulb screwed in, exposing a heavy cardboard tube that served as insulation. This, too, was blackened on one side.

"Uh-huh." Mack pulled up the cardboard sleeve and prodded a loose wire jammed underneath it. "That's your problem."

"The wire?" Faith asked. "Where's it supposed to be attached?"

Mack grabbed a screwdriver from his tool belt and pointed to a small screw on one side. "Right there. It should be hooked up like this other one is. Those two wires are the end of the cord that goes through the base and out the bottom of the lamp and plugs into the wall."

Wolfe studied it for a moment. "How could that wire have gotten loose and twisted up under the insulating sleeve?"

"It couldn't have," Mack stated. "Not without some help."

Faith and Wolfe both stared at him.

"With that wire stuffed down there against the metal of the fixture, that whole lamp would be electrified. 'Course the 110 volts from your usual outlet wouldn't be enough to do more than give somebody a good zap. Not unless he was standing in water or something."

Wolfe's expression was grim. "Like in a full bathtub."

"That'd do it." Mack snapped his fingers. "Just like that."

"There's no chance it was an accident?" Wolfe asked.

"None. If it was only a case of bad workmanship—and I know the manor don't put any junk in the rooms—the first person to turn it on however many years ago would have known it right then. This ain't a matter of wear and tear. No sir."

Faith pressed her lips together. If the lamp had been deliberately tampered with, then there could be no doubt that someone had also tampered with the salad dressing. Whether or not Camilla thought the idea was ridiculous, someone was trying to hurt her, maybe even kill her.

"You want me to go ahead and rewire it?" Mack asked.

"No, I want you to leave it just like it is," Wolfe replied. "Is there somewhere you can lock it up for now?"

"Yeah. I got an old steamer trunk that'll do. There's a sturdy lock on it."

"Good. Put on some gloves and handle the lamp as little as possible while you're locking it up."

Mack considered for a moment. "My fingerprints are all over it already. Two or three others I expect too."

"That's okay. There's nothing we can do about that now. But if there's anyone else's prints, we don't want to smudge them." Wolfe stopped for a minute. "Is there something you could put that cardboard piece in for me?"

The old man opened a drawer and took out a box of sandwich bags. "That do? I use 'em to keep things sorted out."

"Just right." Wolfe used the screwdriver to lift the cardboard tube off the table and into the bag. Then he sealed the bag. "Put the rest of the lamp in your trunk, and don't let anyone know where it is."

Mack nodded. "I'll see to it."

"What are you going to do?" Faith asked Wolfe once they were back upstairs.

One side of his mouth turned up the slightest bit. "I was considering what Mack said about how many people could have touched that lamp before it shorted out. I'm sure housekeeping has polished it several times, but there could still be all kinds of fingerprints on it."

"Innocent fingerprints," Faith said.

"Exactly. But if there are any fingerprints on that insulating cardboard tube, they would have to belong to someone who had actually disassembled the lamp and detached that wire, not merely an innocent passerby. I thought maybe Andy Garris could have somebody check it for prints."

"You think we should involve the police?"

Wolfe shrugged. "I wouldn't quite say 'involve' yet. Nothing serious has happened, and we don't have any evidence against anyone at this point. But I do want to tell the chief what's happened and see what we should do."

"Good. I'd feel terrible if something more serious occurred and we hadn't tried to stop it."

Wolfe nodded. "If there are prints on that cardboard, then he can question whoever they belong to. And even if there aren't, maybe a bit of police presence will discourage whoever is behind these incidents."

Faith exhaled, surprised by how relieved she felt knowing the police would soon be looking into matters. "I have a feeling Camilla's not going to like being inconvenienced."

"She'd be a lot more inconvenienced if she wound up dead," Wolfe said grimly.

"True. I feel bad for the finalists, though. They have enough stress right now just trying to get their entries done without being interrogated by the police too."

"It must be done. Besides, one of them might be more interested in getting to Camilla than actually winning the contest. If that's the case, then we want him—"

"Or her," Faith supplied as they stepped into the lobby.

"Or her," Wolfe repeated, "to know we're looking out for Camilla. And maybe preventing anything else from happening is better than finding the guilty party."

Alex was striding across the gallery toward them. "There you are. Sorry to interrupt you two, but could I get into the library?"

"Sure." Faith glanced at her watch. It still wasn't her usual opening time. "What can I help you with?"

Wolfe smiled politely. "If you'll excuse me, I'll go see to this little matter we were discussing."

"Please keep me posted," Faith said. "I really want to know."

"I'll be in touch when I find out something." Wolfe nodded to the other man. "Alex."

As soon as Wolfe was gone, Faith and Alex started walking toward the library.

"How are things going with your entry?" Faith asked.

He shrugged. "All right, I guess. I had what I thought was a great plot twist, but now I'm wondering if I read it in one of Heyer's books."

"Is that really a problem? I've always heard that there are only so many plots out there anyway."

Alex gave her a reluctant grin. "Maybe. I guess it's all about what you do with them in your own story. Still, I've got a feeling that I read this one somewhere, and I want to make sure what I have in mind is different enough so it doesn't look as if I lifted it in its entirety."

When they got to the library, Faith rummaged in her purse, found her keys, and unlocked the door. "Do you know which book you're wondering about?"

"That's the problem. I can't remember if it was *The Convenient Marriage* or *Sylvester*. It wasn't much, something in one of the subplots, and I'm fairly sure it influenced me, but that's not the same thing as plagiarism, is it?"

"I wouldn't think so." She led him over to where the Regency romances were shelved and found the books he wanted. "By the time you make it work for your own plot, it should be different enough."

"Thanks." He took the books from her and hesitated.

"Is there anything else I can help you with?" she asked.

"No. Thanks again." Alex took a few steps toward the door and then turned back again. "Actually, yeah. I was wondering how Camilla is doing. Have you seen her?"

"I talked to her last night, and she seemed to be fine. She still refused to see a doctor. Whatever triggered her allergy evidently wasn't strong enough to give her a particularly bad reaction, but I'm sure it gave her quite a scare."

"You didn't happen to talk to Giselle too, did you? I mean, I suppose she was pretty frightened, seeing her mother like that."

"I'm sure she was. And, yes, I did see her last night." Faith wondered if she should tell him that Camilla knew about his past relationship with Giselle. She decided it wasn't her place to inform him, and it probably wouldn't help the situation anyway. It might make it difficult for him to concentrate on his entry. Even more so than knowing Giselle was here in the first place.

"Is Giselle all right?" There was definitely concern in his voice, his eyes, and every line of his face.

"I believe so," Faith said, "though I imagine she'd be more all right if you would talk to her for a minute or two."

Alex's expression was nonchalant and impenetrable. "Whatever it was that Giselle and I had is over, and I can't afford to think about it now." He held up the books. "This is what I came for. Anything that doesn't have to do with the contest will have to wait until Friday night. So, thanks for your help. I'll try not to bother you again."

"No, really, it's no bother at all. I'm happy to do what I can."

The words weren't even out of her mouth before he was gone.

Faith didn't care what he said. Whatever he and Giselle had was certainly not over. Not yet.

She thought again about the lamp that had been tampered with. Someone was trying to get to Camilla. Or maybe the guilty party was more interested in hurting her to get to someone close to her.

Faith hoped Wolfe would return from the police station soon.

10

That morning all the contestants were in and out of the library seeking Faith's help with various aspects of research. Faith found the variety of questions they asked interesting and even rather daunting. What did a lady of the ton eat for breakfast? What was the most outrageous hairstyle of the day? What did the number of capes on a gentleman's greatcoat signify? Could a respectable lady attend a rout, and how was that affected by the presence of her husband?

Each finalist understood how important it was to get every period detail correct. Readers of the genre were always aware when something wasn't accurate, and they were sure to let publishers and authors know about it. An error as to the style of a cravat or the meaning of a lady's fan could cost one of the contestants a book contract, and none of them was going to be outdone by the others.

By lunchtime, Faith's head was spinning. It was a fascinating subject, but there were so many things to know that she was amazed that any writer ever got it right.

As she headed back to the cottage through the garden, she heard voices from the other side of a tall hedge. She couldn't quite make out the words, but she could tell it was a man and a woman. When she got closer to the end of the hedge, she realized the man was Tony. The couple came into sight, and it didn't surprise her that the woman was Melanie. She was laughing.

"Hello, you two," Faith called. "I didn't expect to see you out here."

"I'm dying being cooped up in my room all the time," Melanie said. "I had to get outside for a while, so I went to the beach."

"The weather's beautiful today," Faith commented.

"It is. I spend a lot of time on the beach at home, especially when I'm writing."

"California, right?" Faith asked.

Melanie beamed at her. "Discovery Bay. It's about sixty miles from San Francisco."

"How about you?" Faith asked, turning to Tony. "Where are you from?"

He blinked. "Oh, I live in New York City. Not too far from the office."

"But you're not from there," she said lightly. "At least that's not what your accent says."

"Get outta heyah! Not from New Yawk? Fuhgeddaboudit!"

Faith couldn't help but laugh at Tony's over-the-top accent.

His usual charming smile touched his lips. "Actually, I've lived all over, but New York is home right now."

"I don't suppose California is one of those 'all over' places?" she asked with a playful glance at Melanie. "You two seem to know each other."

"Oh, a little," Melanie said. "We met a couple of months ago in Dallas."

He nodded. "I was with Ralph at a writers conference there, and Melanie had an appointment to pitch to him."

"Ralph didn't ask me to send in my full manuscript," Melanie admitted, "and I wasn't allowed to tell him about my entry in the contest. But Tony and I talked for a few minutes while I was waiting for my appointment."

"I was a bit surprised to see her here," Tony said, "especially since we already got a chance to talk at the conference in Minneapolis and the workshop in Portland. But publishing's a small world, and you're pretty much guaranteed to see a great many people you've met before."

Faith nodded but did not comment.

"Anyway, this coast is nice for a change." Melanie caught her wind-whipped blonde hair in both hands and twisted it into a makeshift knot. "The beach is different here, but there's something about the sound of the ocean that helps me think."

"It's so relaxing," Faith said. "I can hear it from my cottage, and it lulls me right to sleep."

"I probably won't have time to sleep until Friday," Melanie said ruefully. "There's too much to do."

"You've got to sleep," Tony said solicitously. "Ralph wants you all to rest well and have enough to eat."

"I know." She grinned at him.

"That's why he sent me round to fetch her in to lunch," he told Faith, and then he smiled suddenly. "I'm sure you're welcome to join us."

"No thanks. You two go on. I live in the gardener's cottage on the grounds, and I have some things I need to do at home during lunch. But I'll be back in the library in about an hour, so let me know if you need anything."

Tony and Melanie set off for the manor, and Faith continued her walk. She had just reached her front door when her cell phone rang. Surprised to see it was Wolfe, she answered.

"Listen, can you return to the house right away?" he asked. "I have Andy with me, and he wants to talk to everybody about what's been going on."

"What did you find out about the lamp?"

"We've already been down to see Mack. Besides his fingerprints, that insulation tube was wiped clean."

The cat watched from the branches of a potted tree, curious about what the human was doing, kneeling there on the hallway floor. Why would anyone want to make those little metal things stick out of the doorframe? Maybe there was supposed to be something tied to them. Humans sometimes used metal things like that to hang stuff on the wall, especially those fascinating shiny things they put up in the winter

when they had secret packages and trees inside the house. But those were normally much higher up, at least at a human's eye level, and often closer to the ceiling than that, and they weren't usually this small. These were close to the floor. Even the cat would have to lean down a bit to see them.

As far as he could see, there were two metal things, one on either side of the door. Surely there would be something hung on them now, but that never happened. Instead the human looked at them for a moment and then hurried away.

The cat leaped to the floor and sauntered up to the door. This was the room where the dog stayed most of the time. Maybe these little metal things had something to do with her, but they didn't have her smell on them, only the smell of human.

It was puzzling.

Faith returned to the manor and joined Wolfe and the others who were meeting with Chief Garris.

Camilla still insisted that there was no reason for anyone to try to harm her. Ralph and Tony appeared grave and apprehensive. Jenny, holding Emma tightly in her arms, seemed bewildered. Giselle sat at her mother's side, looking at everyone else warily.

The chief questioned the three finalists at length. Tall, bald, and still fit in his late fifties, Garris would have been intimidating if it weren't for the calmness in his deep voice and the kindness in his blue eyes.

The three finalists answered the chief's questions with a touch of impatience, no doubt begrudging the valuable minutes he was taking from their already limited writing time.

The chief's questioning brought no new information to light. No one knew anything about the lamp or the salad dressing. Eventually Garris dismissed everyone, merely giving them all a stern warning that any further incidents would trigger a full-scale investigation and hours of questioning down at the station.

Later in the afternoon, Faith went down to the kitchen. Since it was between lunch and dinner, she hoped she'd find Brooke alone and able to talk for a moment. As she had expected, Garris had already spoken to her friend about the meal the night before.

"I told him what I told you," Brooke said. She was preparing chocolate baklava. "I made that dressing myself, and it didn't leave my hands until I set it on the tray to go up to the banquet hall. That's all I know about it." She finished with the hazelnuts she had been chopping, scraped them into a bowl, and began chopping up semisweet chocolate chips. "Someone tampering with the lamp sounds kind of serious."

"It is serious. And scary. I'll tell you something else too." Faith looked behind her, wanting to be sure they weren't overheard.

Brooke stopped chopping. "What?"

"There's something about Tony that—oh, I don't know. It just doesn't quite ring true."

"What do you mean?"

"I'm not sure. Melanie's from California. Even if she didn't have that sun-bleached hair and deep tan, you could tell it from the way she talks."

Brooke laughed and resumed chopping.

"You can tell Camilla's from the South, Ann's from New York or New Jersey, and Alex comes from somewhere in the Midwest. But Tony . . ." Faith shrugged.

"Tony doesn't really have an accent."

"Exactly. But then again some of the things he says make me wonder. Earlier I saw him and Melanie coming up from the beach. He said Ralph had sent him 'round to fetch her in to lunch.' And he said something about seeing 'a great many people' at writers conferences. Does that sound like a New Yorker to you?"

"Not really."

"At first I thought he just had a charming, old-fashioned way of talking, but when Camilla had that reaction at dinner, he asked if she should be 'going to hospital,' instead of going to *the* hospital. He might have a perfect American accent, but those aren't American phrases."

"What do you think he is? English? Welsh?"

"Could be. He might even be Australian or South African. I don't know. He says he's lived all over, and I didn't press him for details, but you'd think if he was from one of those places, he'd have the accent too."

"Oh!" Brooke abruptly slapped her knife down on the cutting board and hurried to the sink.

"What is it?"

"Wow!" She quickly washed her hands. "What if he is?"

"What if he's what?"

Brooke dried her hands on her apron and then snatched her phone from a shelf above the counter. With a quick swipe and a few touches to her screen, she found what she wanted. It was a blog called *Tattle and Scandal and Dirt—Oh My!*

Faith sighed.

"No, wait," Brooke insisted as she swiped through a variety of sensationally titled posts. "I told you about the baronet who disappeared so he wouldn't have to marry the woman his aunt picked out for him. What if he's the one? What if he's Tony?"

"Don't be ridiculous."

"It could be. That's him with Phillipa Lambton." Brooke showed Faith a picture of a haughty-looking young woman with a long face wearing a riding habit. The man next to her, also dressed for riding, had his face turned away from the camera and one hand up to pull down the brim of his cap.

"I can't tell anything from that."

Brooke scrolled down the blog post. "Look at this picture. It's an old one, but it could be Tony, right?"

Faith examined the photograph of eight or ten young men in

dark blue at the front of a crowd gathered on a riverbank. The caption, dated six years earlier, said, *Clifford Leigh-Smithfield (second from left) and friends, University Boat Race.*

The man second from left was certainly tall and athletic like Tony, but so were all the others. Also, along with the others, he was wearing sunglasses and a cap of some kind and was evidently cheering.

"Don't they have a better picture than that?" Faith asked.

"Apparently, they had to scrounge around for that one. The baronet doesn't like having his picture published." Brooke looked intrigued. "They probably had to pay off one of the other guys in the picture to get it. But come on. It could be him!"

Faith studied the photo again. "I don't know. I guess it could. So could four or five of the others." She pointed. "Look at that one and that one. At least they have dark hair. Your guy's blond."

Brooke rolled her eyes. "Hello. Hair dye."

"I guess that would be easy enough," Faith said, squinting at the picture one more time. "I'm not sure I see it."

"Listen to this." Brooke scrolled from the photo to the article. "'Lady Antoinette Leigh-Smithfield, Duchess of Farrellsmoor, declined comment regarding the whereabouts of her nephew Clifford Leigh-Smithfield when she was seen leaving Buckingham Palace following the gala held there for the Welsh National Opera. Lady Phillipa Lambton, former fiancée of the baronet, has made no statement beyond the official one already released, merely repeating that the engagement was ended by mutual consent. However, sources tell us that her ladyship has been seen enjoying London nightlife with a number of eligible men, including a certain earl whose divorce became final only a week ago.'"

"Okay, what does that prove?" Faith asked. "We knew that already."

"No, listen. 'And despite numerous sightings of Lady Lambton in Paris and Monte Carlo on the arm of the young Duke of Hundsford, Clifford still hasn't been seen in London or at Downings, the family home in Berkshire. People are wondering where he is and when he will return.' See? Why couldn't he be Tony? He'd have had plenty of time to come to New York and get a job under a fake name."

Faith looked at her dubiously. "I don't know how easy that would be."

"If he has connections, I bet he could. Lords and stuff like that don't have to play by the rules."

"I thought he was a baronet."

"Whatever." Brooke read on. "'Clifford's certainly staying out of sight, though reliable sources have only recently divulged that he and several of his mates have spent the past few months at—'" Her mouth turned down. "Oh."

"Yes?" Faith asked, not quite hiding a smile. "Where is he?"

"'At the New Zealand home of his longtime friend Andrew deVille, son of the French financier,'" Brooke finished, sounding more than a little disappointed.

"Does it say anything about him working for a pittance in New York?"

Brooke scowled at her. "Oh, hush."

"It was an interesting theory anyway. What was so bad about Lady Phillipa that Clifford had to hide somewhere halfway around the world?"

"Some people say he didn't like having to always be at some event or other or having reporters following him around, and she loves the party scene." Brooke pointed at a picture of Phillipa in an enormous black-and-white hat. "That was at Ascot. Pictures of her are all over the Internet, mostly with the upper crust, a lot of times with one of the royals."

"She *is* nobility, I suppose. What else would she do?"

"I don't know, but it looks like that's not what Clifford wanted. Or maybe he simply didn't like his aunt telling him who to marry."

Faith shrugged. "If he's just a baronet and she's the daughter of a duke or an earl or whatever she is, it would be a step up for him, but I can understand why he might not like it. He probably wasn't used to having all that attention after their engagement was announced."

"All I'm saying is that it would have been much more romantic if he was here in disguise." Brooke went back to her baklava, measured out sugar and cinnamon, and stopped again. "Or maybe he infiltrated Northanger Press so he could get rid of Camilla because she's planning to write a tell-all book about his family."

"Who says she's writing a tell-all book?" Faith demanded. "That's not even her genre."

"Well, he wouldn't care if she was only working on another Regency, would he?"

"Or maybe he's actually in New Zealand and hoping people will leave him alone."

"You're no fun," Brooke said.

Some of the kitchen staff came in to start preparing for dinner, and Faith headed to the library. She couldn't help the tiniest of grins when she spotted Tony in the lobby.

"Hello again," he said. "You haven't seen Camilla anywhere ab—around, have you?"

She was sure he had almost said *about* instead of *around*. Exactly who was he? And could he possibly have any reason to do away with Camilla? It seemed absurd.

"Not since lunch," Faith said. "Is something wrong?"

"Not at all." Tony held up a paper bag with *Happy Tails Gourmet Bakery* printed on it. "She sent me out for something special for Emma. The two of them were in the crafts room. Painting, if you'd like to call it that."

"Really?"

"It looked mostly like Camilla was dribbling paint on the canvas and then letting Emma walk on it. They both seemed to be having a lovely time, though."

"Yes, it sounds like it." Faith paused, then gave him a guileless smile. "So how did you happen to end up working for Northanger Press? Are you planning to become an editor eventually?"

Tony shook his head, amusement in his blue eyes. "I fell into it. I was visiting a friend in New York, and he told me about Northanger. I thought it would be fun. You know, traveling here and there, meeting famous authors."

"Going out to get doggy treats," Faith teased.

"It's not glamorous, but it's a good, steady job. I like it." He chuckled. "I suppose half the fun is never knowing what will happen next."

"Have you worked for Ralph long?"

"Oh, I don't know. Three or four months."

"And before that?" Faith asked, careful to keep her tone casual. "Did you work for another publisher?"

"Actually, about two years ago—"

He was cut off by a shrill scream and a thud from somewhere above them on the second floor.

Faith looked up. "What was that?"

"We'd better go see."

Tony sprinted up the stairs, Faith right behind him. A short hallway led from the stairway to the Jane Austen Suite where Camilla was staying, and there was already a commotion coming from that direction.

When they turned the corner, Ralph and Ann were helping Camilla stand. Jenny was holding Emma, and Melanie and Alex were standing beside her, all looking on.

Giselle burst out of her own room next to the Jane Austen Suite. "Mother!"

"It's all right," Ralph soothed. "Are you okay, Camilla? Let me help you back into your room."

"What happened?" Giselle pushed past everyone else to get to her mother. "Are you hurt?"

"I'm fine." Camilla turned her palms up. They were both red, no doubt burned on the carpet when she fell. "I don't know what happened. My feet just flew out from under me."

Faith went to her. "Are you sure you're not hurt anywhere? A fall like that can cause damage."

Camilla frowned and rubbed one knee. "I guess I'm a little skinned up, but it's nothing serious. I don't know how I could have been so clumsy." She glanced over at Jenny. "I'm glad I wasn't carrying Emma."

"Oh, me too," Jenny said, cuddling the little dog.

Camilla flinched. "I can't imagine what I did, but my ankle hurts something fierce."

Once Ralph had settled her in a chair back in her room, Camilla crossed her legs and reached down to rub her right ankle. Then she made a soft hiss of pain. She pulled up her pant leg a few inches, revealing a thin, red welt.

Faith bent down to get a closer look, then stared at Camilla. "The only thing I can think of that would make a mark like that is a trip wire."

Ralph studied the welt on Camilla's shin. "What else could have done it?"

Camilla bit her lip, for once appearing afraid. "I didn't see anything. I don't see anything now."

Everyone glanced back toward her open door. There didn't seem to be any wires there or anything else that might have made her trip.

"What did it feel like?" Faith asked.

"I don't know. It all happened so fast. One minute I was walking, and the next I was on the floor." Camilla threw up both hands in dismay and then winced and clutched her left wrist.

"Did you hurt your wrist too?" Giselle asked. "Maybe we should have it x-rayed."

"No balking this time," Ralph said. "It's already swelling. Tony will drive us."

"Of course." Tony gave Giselle a sympathetic look. "I'm sure you'd like to go along."

Giselle nodded, her eyes bright with unshed tears. "Thank you."

Alex glanced at him, and then he took Giselle's arm. "Do you want me to come with you?"

Her expression was cool. "I'm sure you don't have time to sit around a hospital waiting room."

"No, I don't," Alex said with a faint grimace. "If you'll all excuse me, I'd better get back to work on my entry." He stalked out of the room.

Camilla turned to her daughter. Clearly, she wanted an explanation of that little exchange. But before she could say anything, her face twisted with pain and she clutched her wrist again. "I think you're right, Ralph. Maybe we'd better go now."

"I hope it's nothing serious," Ann said politely. "But if you don't need me, I should get to work. I'm behind as it is."

"Me too." Melanie smiled at Tony and then at Camilla. "You be careful, okay?"

Camilla nodded.

As Ann and Melanie left, Ralph helped Camilla up and escorted her to the door. Tony and Giselle followed them out.

Jenny watched them go, deep concern on her wan face. Emma squirmed and whined in her arms. "I'm glad Camilla doesn't seem to be really hurt. But who would have done something like that?"

"I have no idea," Faith answered. "Did you see anything Camilla might have tripped over in the hall?"

Jenny shook her head.

"Was she carrying anything that could have made her stumble or made her not see something in her way?"

"I don't think so."

Frowning, Faith went out into the hallway and knelt down at the door to the Jane Austen Suite. There didn't seem to be anything unusual about the door or the threshold. She pulled the door to and then pushed it open again, and it swung easily into the room. If there was a trip wire or something similar, it must have been set up in the hallway.

She ran her fingers lightly over the doorframe about six inches off the floor, about the height where Camilla's shin had been cut. At first she didn't find anything, but then she noticed a slightly rough spot in the highly polished wood. She leaned closer, squinting.

It was a little hole, hardly an eighth of an inch across, a white speck in the dark stain. A screw hole. Fresh. Not deep. A trip wire didn't have to stay in place once the intended victim walked into it. All it had to do was make the victim stumble. And if it wasn't firmly attached, so much the better for whisking away the evidence in the confusion that would follow. It didn't take long for her to find a corresponding hole on the other side of the doorframe.

Jenny, still holding Emma, joined Faith at the door.

"Where were you when Camilla fell?" Faith asked, standing up.

"I was in my room," Jenny replied. "I couldn't find Emma's stuffed rabbit, and I thought maybe she had left it in there when we were playing last night. I had already searched all over Camilla's room for it."

"And it was in your room?"

"In the bathroom," Jenny said. "Emma had dropped it into one of my shoes in there. I was about to go back to Camilla's room and tell her we'd found it when I heard Camilla scream. I almost tripped myself trying to catch Emma and get out to the hall." She smiled wryly. "I did manage to bang my shin on one of the chairs."

"Was anyone already there when you got out to Camilla?"

"Everyone but you and Tony, and you got there pretty soon after. Giselle was coming out of her room too." Jenny toyed with one of Emma's fluffy ears. "Everything happened so fast."

"It was fast," Faith agreed. "Don't you think it's a little strange how everyone got there so quickly?"

"All the rooms are at this end of the building. I suppose any of them could have heard what happened and come to see, like I did."

"True," Faith said, though she wasn't quite sure that explained everything. "Did you see anyone take anything from by the door? Near Camilla?"

Jenny's forehead wrinkled. "Like what?"

"Anything she could have tripped over, especially a wire or something that could have left a mark like that on her shin."

"No, but it was confusing with everybody crowding around and talking at the same time."

Before Jenny could say anything more, Emma started squirming, barking, and trying to jump down. The tiny dog was determined to get to the braided ficus tree in a large ceramic pot beside the door to the Jane Austen Suite.

Faith didn't have to investigate to know what—or who—was back there. "Watson, come out here right now."

Two black ears and a pair of bright green eyes appeared over the rim of the pot and then vanished.

"Watson," she repeated, "I told you not to tease the guests. That's very bad."

Jenny giggled. "Emma hasn't had this much excitement since one of Camilla's fans broke into her house and tried to steal her hair dryer."

Faith couldn't help laughing. "That must have been interesting."

Emma continued to squirm and bark.

Watson did not come out of his hiding place.

"Okay, Rumpy," Faith said in a stern voice that never seemed to make her cat take her seriously. "If you won't come out, I'll have to come get you."

This time Watson peeped around the side of the pot and crouched down, preparing to make a run for it. He had something shiny in his mouth.

"Don't let him get past you," Faith said to Jenny, keeping her voice low and even. "I'll try to get on his other side." She took one step.

Watson bolted out of his hiding place and down the hall, dragging a long, glittering wire after him.

An instant later, Emma wriggled out of Jenny's arms and darted after him.

"Emma!" Jenny ran after them both.

Faith followed. "Watson, I mean it. Watson!"

The cat fairly flew down the stairs, his prize jangling after him.

But Emma's little legs weren't up to the challenge. After carefully navigating the first step, she stood there yapping and growling until Jenny snatched her up, kissing and scolding her at the same time.

Watson was nowhere to be seen.

Instead, Marlene stood at the bottom of the stairs glaring up at Faith. "What is going on?"

Faith cringed. Marlene was not a fan of noise and commotion, especially inside the manor.

"You're supposed to keep that cat of yours under control when he's here." Marlene scowled when Faith reached her. "We don't need another accident."

"I guess you've already heard about what happened to Camilla," Faith said.

"It's our fault," Jenny said as she joined them. She held the dog close. "Emma saw Watson behind that big pot upstairs and started barking, and that scared him."

Faith fought to keep a straight face. Watson wasn't the least bit afraid of dogs, especially dogs that were no bigger than cotton balls.

Marlene's severe expression relaxed. "I'm sorry Emma was upset by him. Is she all right?"

The little dog sat contentedly in Jenny's arms, looking as if she wanted to know what the next game would be.

"She's fine," Jenny said, "but I think we ought to go upstairs and rest. When Camilla gets back, she'll want to see Emma first thing."

The scowl returned to Marlene's face as soon as Jenny and Emma were gone. "Faith, really, our guests—"

"I'm sorry," Faith said, "but did you see where Watson went?"

"That cat is your business. Mine is making sure our guests aren't disturbed by his foolishness."

"This isn't foolishness," Faith insisted. "He could have a very important piece of evidence."

"What kind of evidence?"

"Just tell me which way he went. I'll explain in a minute, but I don't want him to get away. Did you see him?"

"He ran past me into the gallery. What do you mean about—?"

Faith didn't wait for Marlene to finish. She hurried into the gallery and found Watson sitting at the foot of the statue of Agatha Christie that stood in its center. If he had had more than a stub of a tail, she was certain that it would have been wrapped demurely around his feet. He looked as if her appearance was an unexpected but pleasant surprise.

She glared at him. "All right, mister, where is it? What did you do with that wire?"

Watson extended one back foot and began daintily grooming it.

He squawked when she seized him and unceremoniously lifted him off the floor. There was nothing under him.

"Is this what you're looking for?" Marlene held out a long wire with a small eye screw dangling from each end. "He left it under the arch between here and the lobby, along the edge of one of the carpets."

No wonder Faith hadn't seen it.

"That's it." She took the wire, examining it. "That's it exactly."

"Now you'd better come into my office. I want to know what's going on here."

Faith sighed. "I wish I knew. What I do know isn't enough to have to go to your office about. You did hear about Camilla?"

"I was told that she tripped." Marlene narrowed her eyes. "You don't think the manor could be held responsible?"

"No, I'm sure it couldn't. I'm almost positive this wire was fastened in front of her door so she would trip when she came out." Faith balanced a squirming Watson on one hip and touched one of the screws. It was the perfect size to fit into those shallow little holes in the doorframe of the Jane Austen Suite. "She's not hurt, at least not badly, but this was definitely not an accident."

"I suppose Chief Garris will have to be informed." Marlene looked down her pointed nose at Faith. "Do you want me to handle it? Or do you think you could take care of it yourself? Discreetly."

"We'd better let Wolfe know about it too, don't you think?"

Marlene gave a grudging nod.

"Let me take Watson home, and then I'll see if I can have a word with Wolfe and Chief Garris about this."

Faith left a grumbling Watson on the sofa in the living room at the cottage and locked the front door behind her, even though it wouldn't do any good.

She was walking through the gallery toward the library to call Wolfe when she saw him coming in. It took her only a minute to catch him up on the morning's events.

"It would have been easy for almost anyone to push this out of the way," Wolfe said, inspecting the wire. "And I think you're right. These screws are too short to go very deep. The wire was meant to pop loose as soon as someone tripped over it. We'll have to get Andy back over here."

Faith nodded.

"Any idea who was in a position to have done this?"

"Anybody who was there right after Camilla tripped," Faith said. "I saw Ralph and Ann helping her stand when Tony and I got there. Giselle was just leaving her room next door and coming up to them when we got there. All the others were there too."

"I guess that rules out Giselle and Tony."

Faith frowned. "I don't know if it does. Either of them could have rigged that wire and then waited for Camilla to fall. As long as the culprit was there during the commotion and had a chance to stash the wire behind that planter, it could have been anyone. Though I suppose it couldn't have been Tony after all. He'd been at Midge's bakery getting a treat for Emma. If that wire had been set up before he went out, Jenny would have been the one to trip when she took Emma to her room to find a stuffed rabbit."

"Someone must have known Jenny was out of the room and worked fast. Unless . . ." Wolfe considered for a moment. "Unless whoever it was had already put these eye screws in the doorframe. It would take only a few seconds to string the wire once the screws were in place." There was concern in his blue eyes. "Maybe we'd better figure out where everyone was right before this happened and who got to Camilla's door first. Who went to the hospital with Camilla?"

"Only Ralph and Giselle. Tony drove them."

"That means our three contestants and Jenny are still here."

"Right."

"Perhaps we should do a little sleuthing before we talk to Andy," Wolfe suggested.

Faith smiled.

12

Faith and Wolfe decided to start their questioning with Alex.

"I wouldn't generally repeat this sort of thing," Faith told Wolfe, "but it might have something to do with what's been going on with Camilla. If Alex has a grudge against Giselle because she broke up with him, he might try something like this."

"Or even because she wouldn't give him an in with her mother," Wolfe added.

"But it would be foolish of him to try to sabotage Camilla just when he was about to get his big chance. If something happens to her, then nobody gets a contract. At least not on Friday."

"By that logic, we have to rule out all three of the finalists."

"Unless," Faith said as she knocked on Alex's door, "one of them thinks getting back at Camilla is more important than winning the contest."

"Go away!" Alex barked from inside the room. "I'm busy!"

Faith glanced at Wolfe and then knocked again. "I'm sorry to bother you. It's Faith Newberry and Wolfe Jaxon. We need to talk to you for a minute."

There was a long moment of silence and then a groan. After another moment, the door swung open. Alex scowled at both of them. "Look, I don't mean to be rude, but I'm never going to get this done if I can't have a little peace and quiet. It's a nearly impossible task as it is."

"We need to get a few things straight about what you saw this morning," Wolfe said, smiling as he nudged the door open wider.

Alex exhaled heavily. "Sure. Why not? I have nothing better to do." He stepped back to let them in, then seemed to notice the riot of books and papers on every flat surface in the room. "Sit wherever."

Wolfe cleared off a couple of chairs, and then he and Faith sat down.

"We'll get right to the point," Faith said. "We need to know what you heard that made you come over to Camilla's room, who was there when you got there, and who came afterward."

Alex shrugged. "I was going to go downstairs to get a snack. But mostly to stretch my legs. Up till then, I don't think I'd even gotten out of my chair since about three this morning. Anyway, I was about halfway to the stairs when I heard a scream, so I scrambled back the other way. Camilla was sprawled on the floor. Ann and Ralph were coming from the opposite direction, and Melanie was behind them a few seconds later. Then Camilla's daughter and her assistant arrived pretty soon after that."

"Which one got there first?" Wolfe asked.

"Don't know. I don't think I particularly noticed." Alex nodded at Faith. "You and Ralph's assistant came up too."

"Yes," Faith said. "When we arrived, Jenny was already there, and Giselle was running down the hall."

"There's nothing else I can tell you. I didn't see her fall." Alex tightened his jaw. "I really, *really* don't have time to think about this right now. I don't want to sound callous, but that's the truth. I'm glad Camilla's not seriously hurt, but I don't know what else to say."

Faith glanced at Wolfe. He looked as unimpressed as she felt.

"You didn't notice anything out of place?" Faith pressed. "Something she might have tripped over?"

Alex shook his head.

"Nobody was carrying anything?" Wolfe asked. "Nobody tried to shove something out of the way?"

"Not that I saw." Alex looked at them impatiently.

Faith and Wolfe stood.

"If you think of anything," Wolfe said, "please let us know."

"Right away." Alex rushed them to the door. "Always glad to help."

"Not really," Faith muttered when he had shut the door firmly behind them. "What now?"

"We have one version of the story," Wolfe said. "I guess we can see if everyone else saw it the same way."

Evidently they had. Melanie had been returning to her room after a run on the beach. She couldn't remember who got to the Jane Austen Suite after she did.

Ann had been questioning Ralph about one of the requirements for her contest entry and had been in his room for no more than five minutes. She thought Alex got there after Melanie, but she wasn't positive.

Like Alex, neither of them had seen anything that would have caused Camilla to trip or anyone trying to conceal anything.

By the time Faith and Wolfe had finished talking to the finalists, Camilla, Giselle, Ralph, and Tony had returned from the hospital.

"I told you it wasn't so bad." Camilla grimaced and held up her bandaged wrist. "Thank goodness it's only a sprain."

"And a twisted knee," Giselle mumbled. "And the cut on your shin."

"The doctor said my knee isn't broken or even sprained," Camilla said, "and that cut isn't anything to worry over. I'm more worried about a reporter being there. I'd like to know how they find these things out."

Ralph shook his head as he and Tony helped Camilla up the stairs. Faith, Wolfe, and Giselle followed them.

"Do you feel up to talking for a few minutes?" Faith asked Camilla as the group filed into the author's room.

Camilla nodded. "I'm fine." She smiled at Wolfe. "Please don't think this is a reflection on your beautiful manor."

"Don't you worry about that," Wolfe said with a warm smile of his own. "We just want to make sure everyone is safe."

He and Faith asked each of them about their version of the incident, and with some minor inconsistencies, everyone pretty much told the same story. No one saw anything untoward besides Camilla sprawled on the corridor floor.

Giselle turned to her mother. "If you don't want reporters around, you should refuse to talk to them," she scolded.

"I can't very well do that," Camilla said. "Most of them are nice, and after all, they tell people about my books."

"This had nothing to do with your books," Giselle snapped. "He was an ambulance chaser."

"Who was he?" Faith asked. "Someone local?"

Camilla shrugged. "Where's Jenny? I want Emma in here with me."

"I'll get her," Giselle offered and left the room.

Ralph put his hands on his hips. "The reporter, if you want to call him that, wasn't with any of the papers. No credentials. More likely he's trying to sell stories to the large scandal sheets if he can."

"I guess that'd be worth a lot of money," Faith said.

Ralph nodded. "If the story's big and juicy enough."

"There isn't a story," Camilla said. "I'm clumsy and that's all."

"You know that's not true," Giselle said as she came back into the room with Jenny and Emma.

The small dog whined and squirmed until Jenny set her in Camilla's lap.

"Poor baby," Camilla cooed. "Did we miss her? Of course we did."

"Mother." Giselle's mouth was in a thin line. "You can't ignore this. You didn't get that cut on your shin simply by falling down. Someone must have done it deliberately."

"Now who would do such a thing?" Camilla asked.

"That's what we're trying to figure out," Wolfe said, producing the wire Watson had found.

"What?" Camilla's blue eyes were round with fear. "Where did you get that?"

"It was behind that potted tree next to your door," Faith told her. "Someone must have stashed it there after you fell. It couldn't possibly have been an accident."

"And now it will be all over the news," Ralph said tightly.

Camilla gave him a wan smile. "There's no such thing as bad publicity, is there?"

Ralph's expression softened into genuine fondness. "You always were a trouper. I guess you're right about that, but all the publicity in the world wouldn't do us any good if you aren't around to benefit from it. You're a valuable asset."

Camilla beamed at Ralph.

But Giselle glared at him. "That's my mother, not one of your assets."

Ralph held up both hands in apology. "I didn't mean anything by it. Really. I was only trying to lighten things up. Your mother knows how much everyone at Northanger loves her."

"He didn't mean it like that, honey." Camilla squeezed her daughter's hand. "Come on now. Nothing actually happened."

"It could have." There were sudden tears in Giselle's eyes. "What if someone wants to hurt you? What if someone wants to kill you? You've had three accidents since we got here."

"We're going to do our best to see that nothing like that happens," Wolfe assured her. "I'm planning to talk to our chief of police about it again. For now, Camilla, I don't want you to be left alone. If Giselle and Jenny will take turns keeping you company, I think we'd all feel better about it."

Jenny nodded vigorously. "I should have been here in the first place. Before anything happened."

"Oh, don't be silly," Camilla said. "You left to get Emmie's rabbit. You couldn't have been gone but five or ten minutes."

"It was enough," Giselle said.

Camilla put her hand over her heart. "You're not accusing Jenny, are you?"

Giselle rolled her eyes. "Of course not. I'm only saying she should have been with you. That's her job."

Jenny hung her head.

"I am not an infant," Camilla said. "I don't need constant supervision."

"No one's saying that," Ralph said soothingly, "but constant supervision might not be a bad idea for a while. I think Wolfe's right.

Until we find out what's going on, there's no need to take unnecessary chances. Camilla, this time I have to insist. It won't be for long. You won't mind having Giselle or Jenny with you, will you?"

Camilla sighed. "No, I suppose not. Jenny's always so easy to get along with, but I expect Giselle will quickly become bored."

"I guess we can take turns." Giselle didn't sound thrilled with the prospect. "Better that than worrying about you all the time."

"The only thing you want to do is hide in your room anyway." Camilla glanced meaningfully at Tony. "If you'd like to have someone show you the local sights, I'm sure I wouldn't mind being without you for an hour or two."

Giselle turned red. "Mother."

As usual, Tony made a slight bow. "I'd be quite pleased. Anytime."

"That's all right. Thank you anyway," Giselle told him, then glowered at her mother. "I'd better stay here."

"Come on, Tony," Ralph said. "We should let Camilla get some rest. You ladies let me know if you need anything at all."

"I'm going over to the station to tell Andy about this," Wolfe said, once he and Faith had accompanied Ralph and Tony out of Camilla's room. "I'll let you know what he says. Meanwhile, keep your eyes open." In a few long strides, he was gone.

Ralph turned to Tony. "Did you get those dog treats?"

"Oh yes." Tony patted his pocket and then brought out the bag from Happy Tails. "I completely forgot I had them."

"Okay, good. Maybe that'll make things a little brighter. I have a few contracts to work on, and then I'll need you to make some reservations for Orlando. I'll give you the details when you get through with the dog."

"Right away."

"You've already been a big help, Faith," Ralph said. "I want to know anything else you find out about this business with Camilla."

"I'll do that," Faith promised. "I'm curious, though. What was it you said about a reporter being at the hospital?"

Ralph looked mildly disgusted. "Some guy with a blog. He's local, from what Camilla says, and he's been bugging her for so-called insider information for months now. I guess he saw the press release about the ball and fan event on Friday and assumed she'd be staying here. I don't know how he found out she was in the hospital. He probably has a friend on staff or something. Patient information is supposed to be private, isn't it?"

"Did you get his name?" Faith asked.

Ralph shook his head. "Camilla would know."

"I won't bother her about it right now. I'm sure she just wants to rest for a while."

"I'm sure she does," Ralph agreed. "Excuse me, but I've got to get to work. All this has put me way behind." He disappeared into his room.

"I don't suppose you know who that blogger was," Faith said to Tony.

He smiled his charming smile. "Sorry, no idea. But I know the type. I can't say they're my favorite."

"It sounds like you've had some experience with them," Faith said, keeping her tone light.

Tony laughed. "Me? It's not like I'm a best-selling author. Reporters would find Tony Leigh a pretty dull subject."

She studied him for a moment before deciding to jump in feetfirst. "How about Clifford Leigh-Smithfield?"

13

Tony blinked. "Excuse me?"

"You don't have to answer that if you don't want to." Faith had to struggle to keep her expression neutral. It had been nothing but a crazy shot in the dark, but maybe Brooke had been right after all. "Or perhaps you'd like to tell me about it."

"Follow me." Tony didn't say anything else until he and Faith reached his room and sat down at the table in front of the window.

"Hair dye?" she asked lightly, smiling to herself at the thought of how delighted Brooke would be to know she'd been correct.

Tony immediately put one hand up to his raven locks. "Is it obvious?" he asked in a cultured British voice.

"Not at all. But your hair was blond in the picture I saw."

"How did you find out?"

"I didn't really," Faith admitted. "Not quite, anyway. But once in a while you would say something that made me wonder who you were. And someone showed me your picture on the Internet and told me you had disappeared. Then we saw a blog that said you were in New Zealand."

"I was for a bit, but then I wanted to get away from everything, even my friends. Several of my mates and I are meant to be staying with Drew deVille on the South Island, and I have to admit that Drew's been fabulous in all this. He keeps the nosy parkers at bay, forwards my post to me in New York, and then I send him any replies I might have so he can send them from there. My mobile phone is international, so the few people who have my number don't know where I actually am when they call me."

She shook her head in wonder. "Was it really that bad?"

Tony chuckled. "You mean Phil? No. She simply . . . isn't for me. It's so important to her where she's seen and with whom and how posh the event is. I think she merely thought we looked good together. I can't imagine another reason why she was interested in me."

"So how did all of this happen?"

"Phil told her father she wanted us to marry. I didn't understand how a few rides in the country and an evening or two at the theater could add up to a proposal, but Aunt wouldn't hear of my not proposing once Lord Lambton discussed the terms with her. The two of them believed it would be a grand alliance between our families. I don't know why, since I'm only a baronet and Lord Lambton's an earl, but my family has money and his has spent a touch more than perhaps they ought."

"I guess many old families aren't as well-off as their titles suggest," Faith remarked.

"Aunt told me it would be the making of the family. And I wasn't to spoil it." Tony frowned. "Before I even broached the subject with Phil, she had 'let it slip' to a friend of hers and it got into the paper, so I thought I might as well go ahead with it. Silly me."

"I suppose nobody would possibly guess you're here working at Northanger Press. Is this truly what you want?" Faith asked. "Being an administrative assistant at a publishing house?"

"Not forever. But for now?" Tony shrugged. "As I said before, it's not a bad life. I haven't done this job for very long, but I've already been to a lot of places, met a lot of people, and had a lot of fun. Ralph's a good guy and not hard to work for, and I never have to wonder if people like me because of my title rather than for who I am. One day, when my aunt realizes she can't trade me off to the highest bidder, I'll go back. But today is not that day. Judging by her rather forceful letters to me, she still thinks I can patch things up with Phil and 'make the Leigh-Smithfields proud.' To be honest, I was tired of all of it." He gave her a winsome look.

She had to laugh. "It seems like a pretty extreme thing to do."

"You don't know my aunt," Tony said. "There are very few times she doesn't get her way. Occasionally one must literally go to the ends of the earth to escape her."

"I suppose she holds the purse strings."

"Only until I'm twenty-five so not much longer now. For the present, my friends pretend I'm lazing my life away down under, and my valet gets paid nicely for doing nothing but keeping his mouth shut."

Faith sighed. "It's such a shame."

"Not marrying an earl's daughter?"

"No," she said. "Not using that beautiful accent."

Tony gave her a sly grin. "I suppose that's what gave me away, was it? I didn't quite pull off the American accent?"

"It isn't that. Your accent's remarkably good. It's just that once in a while you use a word or phrase that isn't quite American. I thought you must be from somewhere else, though I didn't suspect you were a runaway groom."

"I'm not as bad as all that," Tony protested. "I did have a quiet chat with Phil. I told her we'd never be happy together and we'd best call off the engagement. She didn't want to. I think it was more a matter of not getting what she wanted rather than being heartbroken, but she seems to be well over it now. If Aunt would drop it, I might go home sooner rather than later. But then again, I might not." He didn't say anything more, but there was a look in his eye that made her wonder.

"Have you told—?" She caught herself before she said Melanie's name. "Have you told Ralph?"

Tony shook his head. "I have a friend at the British embassy who worked out all the papers for me. I'm here legally, though under only a couple of my names. I go by Tony Leigh. Most people assume it's spelled L-e-e, and I don't correct them. My full name is Clifford Antony Swain Leigh-Smithfield."

"Camilla was right. You would make a wonderful hero for one of her Regencies, just for the name alone."

"I wouldn't go so far as that, though I have dropped a word or two in Ralph's ear about some of his writers using Americanisms in their romances set in Britain. Camilla does very well, but some of the others are truly terrible. For instance, gentlemen of the Regency era did not use the word *okay*."

The stern disapproval on his face made her smile. "I'm sure you've saved Northanger Press from endless embarrassment on several occasions."

"I hope so," Tony said, and then he was suddenly serious. "I'd like to know what's going on with Camilla. It's a miracle she hasn't been grievously injured so far."

"I know. You haven't heard anyone say anything suspicious, have you? Or noticed something that didn't look right?"

"Nothing. When we got upstairs after Camilla fell, I was watching her. I didn't think to pay attention to anyone else."

"I guess that's what our perpetrator was counting on." Faith stood. "I'd better get back to work. Our finalists might need to get into the library."

Tony escorted her to the door but didn't immediately open it. "About Lady Lambton and all that . . ."

"Your secret is safe with me, but Brooke is going to be crushed to someday find out that a real baronet was staying here and she didn't even know it."

He laughed and swung the door open. "When that someday comes, I promise I'll send her a box of tea and some genuine English toffee to make it up to her."

Faith saw very little of the three finalists the rest of the day. She assumed they were all furiously writing, trying to compensate for the time they had lost because of what had happened to Camilla earlier.

They had only one day left. Tomorrow was Thursday, and on Friday morning, their entries had to be submitted to Camilla and Ralph, ready or not. Faith didn't envy them in the least. They would have every right to be quite proud of themselves if they managed to finish on time with a captivating entry.

Faith dined at home for a change. Ralph still insisted that his three finalists eat dinner with him and Camilla, but this time it was only a simple meal and not a business meeting. After Faith had paid bills and balanced her checkbook, she was glad to relax with Watson. He seemed content to curl up next to her on the couch while she watched parts of her favorite version of *Pride and Prejudice*, the one with Colin Firth. The scenery was so lovely that it made her want to see it in person.

The thought of England reminded her of Tony. It seemed strange in this day and age that anyone, especially a man, would find it necessary to run from an unwanted marriage, but it sounded like his aunt was quite a formidable woman. Good for Tony that he hadn't let her force him into something that would have made him and Lady Phillipa both unhappy. There were too many miserable marriages as it was.

Faith laughed to herself at the notion of Tony presenting his blue-blooded aunt with laid-back Melanie Wilde. It was obvious that Melanie came from money, but her breezy West Coast manners might be seen as decidedly lowbred to English nobility. Of course, it was far too soon to consider anything of that nature between Tony and Melanie. Even though they had met a few times before, they couldn't possibly know each other very well. But they both seemed interested in remedying that.

Faith stroked the back of Watson's head as he slept next to her. Eyes still closed, he started to purr and knead her leg with his front paws.

As she watched Elizabeth Bennet's amazement when she realized what Mr. Darcy had done to save her family from ruin, she thought about Tony once again. Darcy's actions had been entirely honorable, but Faith couldn't help wondering what a man in love might do for the benefit of his loved one. If Melanie's aim was to take Camilla's place as the queen of Regency romance, then Camilla would have to be put out of the way, wouldn't she? And if Tony could show his devotion to her by clearing Melanie's path, would he?

It still didn't make sense. For one thing, Tony had been out getting dog treats for Emma when Camilla had taken her fall. There was no way that trip wire could have been in place for more than the few minutes Jenny had left Camilla's room to look for Emma's stuffed rabbit. But if Tony and Melanie were in on it together . . .

Faith scratched behind Watson's ear, considering. Tony and Melanie had met at least three times before coming to the manor. Three times that they admitted anyway. But if they worked together behind the scenes, giving each other alibis anytime something happened to Camilla, maybe . . .

No, that couldn't be right. Camilla was Melanie's best chance to get her big break in publishing. Sure, an extremely ambitious person might want to do away with the competition, but the finalists were not competition for Camilla. At least not yet. Not until they had their books published. Camilla would be instrumental in making that first step possible. And Melanie was the only one of the three contestants who didn't seem to have some kind of personal connection to Camilla outside the contest. Could she—?

Watson nipped her hand. It was his indication that she had been scratching him too hard.

Faith stopped and pulled her hand away. "Sorry," she told him, smoothing down his fur. "I was thinking of something else."

He looked annoyed and slunk off the couch, eventually disappearing into the kitchen.

Still preoccupied with what was going on at the manor, she stopped paying much attention to the show and dozed off on the couch.

Faith woke again with a start. It took her a moment to figure out exactly what had disturbed her. There was some kind of crackly noise coming from near the front door. She sat up, blinking blearily, and frowned. "What do you have, Rumpy?"

Watson immediately crouched over the contraband he had been batting around the floor, then scampered into the bedroom with it.

Shaking her head, she stood up and stretched. When she looked down she sighed heavily. Her neatly organized purse, which she had left on the chair near the door, was lying open on the floor with most of the contents scattered around it. "Watson!"

There was no telling what he had taken with him.

"Watson, whatever it is, you'd better give it back right now." Faith strode into the bedroom after him.

He was in the corner with a crumpled piece of paper at his feet, looking not so much guilty as scheming. When she got about halfway across the room, he snatched up the paper and darted into the bathroom.

"Big mistake, Rumpy. Big mistake." She had him cornered.

Watson glanced from side to side, and, seeing there was no way out, he huffed and dropped the paper on the bathroom floor. Then, acting as if he disdained the mere idea of playing with such an unsophisticated toy, he strolled out of the bathroom with his nose in the air.

Faith frowned as she picked up the paper. If it had come from her purse, she didn't recognize it. She might fold a piece of paper before she put it into her purse, but she would never crumple it up into a ball like this. Where had it come from?

She smoothed it out as flat as possible and saw that it was a faintly printed receipt from one of the shops at the airport. She hadn't been to the airport in a long time. Certainly not since she had tidied her purse last week.

What was the receipt for anyway? About a third of it was torn off, but she could see most of the description:

EANUTS @ $1.99 . . . . $9.95.

Five packets of peanuts.

14

"I don't know where it came from or how it got into my purse," Faith told Wolfe when she showed him the torn receipt in the library the next morning. "But it might explain where those peanuts came from that were in the guests' rooms."

He frowned. "It would be easy enough to drop the receipt into your bag when you weren't paying attention."

"I guess so. My purse closes with only one big snap at the top. It's not like it's zipped shut. Anyone could have come up behind me or beside me and slipped something in there. And all the guests came from the airport."

Wolfe took the receipt from her, looking it over again. "Whoever it was paid in cash."

"Of course."

"But why would our perpetrator put it in your purse? Wouldn't it make more sense to get rid of that kind of evidence as quickly as possible? Before even coming to the manor?"

"Definitely," she said. "Unless whoever's behind this wants to incriminate someone else."

"You?"

Faith blinked at him. "I hadn't thought of that. You don't think someone's trying to frame me, do you?"

"No, definitely not," Wolfe said, his blue eyes warm. "Besides, it could have been put there for some other reason. Someone could have realized he still had it in his pocket or something, and he had to get rid of it immediately and inconspicuously. Conversely, maybe someone found it and wanted you to know about it, hoping it would help with the case."

"Then why not just give it to me?"

"I don't know. Maybe this person thought he'd be suspected if he had something like that, or maybe he didn't want to be the one responsible for exposing the guilty party. Or it could be Watson found it somewhere, and it wasn't in your purse at all."

"Now that I can believe. He finds the oddest things to play with. Anyway, however it got to me, it must have something to do with what's been happening to Camilla. What did the chief say about the wire?"

"He took it into custody," Wolfe said. "There weren't any usable fingerprints or identifying marks on it, so he didn't think it was much help in the investigation. But it does make it pretty clear that whatever is going on is no accident. He's going to come by when he can and have a look around, ask a few more questions, that sort of thing. I'll keep the receipt and show it to him then. He agreed that it was a good idea to have someone stay with Camilla for the time being."

Faith was silent for a long moment, and then she tapped her chin with one finger. "What if we've been looking in the wrong place all this time?"

"What do you mean?"

"At first I thought one of the finalists might be behind this, but maybe that's too obvious. Who else might be involved?"

Wolfe shrugged. "If we stick to our contest-related guests, there's Ralph, Tony, Jenny, and Giselle. Who do you suspect?"

"None of them seems very likely. Ralph might not always enjoy having to cater to Camilla's every whim, but she's made Northanger Press extremely successful. I don't think he'd want anything to happen to her."

"Right. He doesn't seem the type. Neither does Tony." Wolfe grinned. "Unless he's tired of her comments about his looks all the time."

"If that's sufficient motive, then we'll have to put you on the suspects list too," Faith teased.

"I haven't had to put up with Camilla for nearly the amount of time Tony has, but then again, I'm not a twenty-something anymore." There was a gleam of humor in his expression. "I've grown to appreciate a nice compliment when I can get it."

Faith doubted that Wolfe was ever short of admirers, even though he was twenty years Tony's senior. "I don't think Tony minds it. At least, not enough to do her any harm." At this point she didn't want to mention wondering about Tony's connection to Melanie. It was a rather dubious chain of logic and completely unsupported by any evidence. "So that leaves us with Jenny and Giselle."

"Hmmm." Wolfe leaned one elbow on the intricately carved arm of the sofa and propped his chin on his fist. "They are both in close contact with Camilla. It wouldn't have been hard for either of them to rig the lamp, set the trip wire, or doctor the salad dressing on Tuesday night. But would they? Giselle is her daughter, and both of them seem too timid to me, especially Jenny."

"True, but those can be the most dangerous ones. Sometimes it's the doormats who take all they can handle and finally snap. But I haven't seen Camilla treat either of them badly. She might be a bit of a drama queen and obviously insists on being center stage all the time, but she hasn't been unkind."

"That you've seen," Wolfe reminded her.

"That I've seen," Faith admitted. "Maybe I should have a chat with them when Camilla isn't around and try to get some answers. But I still don't know what any of these attempts is supposed to accomplish. Giselle and Jenny are dependent on Camilla, and from what I can tell, she gives them both a good life."

"If anything happened to Camilla, Jenny would be looking for a new job. Giselle, on the other hand, stands to inherit a tidy sum. That is, if the celebrity net worth sites have their figures right."

Faith raised her eyebrows. "I never suspected that you'd be interested in that kind of thing. It sounds more like something Brooke would want to know."

"Money's the reason for a lot of things," Wolfe said, looking suddenly grim. "It never hurts to follow that trail when you're searching for answers."

Faith remembered what Wolfe had said about money when Giselle came into the library later that morning.

"Mother wants to know if you have anything on men's military footwear during 1815." She rolled her eyes. "It drives me crazy, having to stay with her every minute, and I don't think she's much enjoying having to be in her room all day, but I doubt that part will last very long."

"She does seem to like keeping busy," Faith commented.

"Don't get me wrong," Giselle said. "It's not that I don't love her and want her to be safe, but I'm about 100 percent introverted. I need alone time to recharge, and the only thing Mother wants to do is chatter."

"I can understand that. My roommate in college was an introvert. She was smart and friendly and really funny when she was with only two or three other people, but she always said being around a lot of people for too long wore her out. And small talk was absolutely exhausting for her."

Giselle nodded and sat on the corner of the desk. "Yeah, it's exactly like that. Some people get all charged up being in a crowd but not me. Just give me some books or embroidery or colored pencils, and I'm good."

"That sounds nice and relaxing." Faith smiled at her, trying to think of some way of broaching the subject of money without sounding too inquisitive. "You know, I don't think I ever heard what you do for a living."

"Not much really. Sometimes I sell a painting or two or have one commissioned. I had a show in a gallery a couple of years ago, but hardly anyone came to it."

"Oh, that's exciting. You must do pretty well to be able to support yourself on your work."

Giselle made a face. "No, I don't make much, but Daddy left me enough money that I don't have to worry about anything. Except for jerks who want to live off me when they find out I have money. But I'm careful."

"That's smart. As long as you don't let it make you cynical."

"Yeah, I know. Mother says I'm not allowed to be cynical about men until I'm forty and an old maid." She froze, eyes widening. "I'm sorry. I didn't mean—uh, not that there's anything wrong with being forty."

Faith smiled. "I'm not going to be cynical about men either. And I'm only thirty-nine."

Giselle's face was flushed, but she smiled too. "Sorry."

"Don't worry about it. And believe me, there really is nothing wrong with being my age. I'm comfortable with myself, I don't worry nearly so much about what other people say and think, and I've figured out what's important to me and what's not. It's a nice place to be." She patted Giselle's arm. "You'll get there in time."

"When I do, I hope I'll be like you." Then Giselle cringed. "If I haven't messed things up too bad by then."

"It's not too late to set things right. Maybe you can talk to Alex tomorrow at the ball," Faith told her. "It's going to be quite an event. I'm sure you've seen the decorations they're putting up now in the Great Hall Gallery."

"It all looks so beautiful, like a real Regency ball. I'm not much for big events like this, but I have the most wonderful dress and jewelry. It's almost like pretending to be someone else. Someone much less awkward than I am."

"You know, that's what many people do when they have to appear in public or give speeches. They pretend to be someone else, and it makes them feel much less self-conscious. I'm sure you'll be absolutely fine, and Alex will be so smitten with you that you won't even think about being nervous."

Giselle gave Faith a shy smile. "Do you think so?"

"I think Alex is too determined to win this contest to show you how he really feels right now. But by tomorrow night he will have turned in his entry, and then he'll have time to think about real life again." Faith had seen the genuine concern on his face when he knew Giselle was upset, no matter how he tried to cover it up later on. "I can't promise you anything about how he feels or what he might say, but I still believe you ought to at least try to find out. It's better to know for sure, even if it doesn't turn out the way you want it to."

"Yeah, I guess. But I don't know what my mother is going to say if I start seeing him again. You might have noticed she's very protective of me. I wonder now if she was wrong when she said he was only using me to get close to her."

"She's the one who told you that?" Faith asked. "I thought it came from an argument you had with Alex."

Giselle winced. "That was after Mother and I talked about him. I was telling her I wanted her to meet him, that I thought he might be the real thing, but when she found out that he wanted to write, especially that he wanted to write Regencies, she said he was a phony. Alex asked who I was at a party and then came over and introduced himself. He told me then that he wanted to meet me because of Mother but not because of anything I could do for him. Just because he was a fan of hers and wanted to chat. Does that seem weird to you?"

"I suppose it could be, but it doesn't have to be. Did he make you feel uncomfortable?"

"A little bit at first," Giselle admitted. "But he was polite and funny and not pushy. We just . . . talked. I didn't think I'd ever see him again, but later I ran into him in a bookstore and went over to say hi. We ended up getting a burger together. That time we didn't talk about Mother at all. It was nice."

Faith thought for a moment. "When you and Alex had your argument, did you tell him what your mother said?"

"Yeah. That made him pretty mad, I think," Giselle replied. "He said I was too old to let my mother run my life, and that's when I told him never to call me again. He texted me once after that."

"What did he say?"

Giselle hung her head. "I don't know. I deleted it without reading it."

Well, that's one way to avoid dealing with the issue. "There's nothing you can do about any of that now," Faith said. "Sometime tomorrow, after he turns in his entry, ask him if he would mind talking to you for a few minutes. Say you're sorry you ended things the way you did, without giving him a chance to tell you his side."

"But I don't know if I want to get back together with him."

"I'm not saying you should tell him that. I don't think you can know until you talk to him. I mean, really talk to him. Without anyone looking over your shoulder."

"And if he's still mad and won't talk to me?" Giselle asked in a small voice.

"Then you'll know he's not the right one for you, and you can stop wondering." Faith gave her an encouraging smile. "And if he does want to talk to you again, won't it be nice to have an escort to the ball?"

Giselle nodded, and then there was a touch of a grin on her full lips. "I don't know what Mother would think if I was to walk in on Alex's arm. That might be the best part of the whole trip."

"She'll be happy for you as long as she knows he wasn't trying to take advantage of you," Faith said. "Won't she?"

"Oh, sure she would. But she's always been a little suspicious of people. She was that way even when Daddy was alive." Giselle exhaled heavily. "I wish there didn't have to be money. It makes people act weird."

"I suppose it does. But if there wasn't actual money, there'd be something else for people to squabble over. It's human nature."

Faith couldn't help thinking of Tony, who'd run halfway around the world to escape being seen as nothing more than a title. He wasn't so much different from Giselle, who obviously wanted to be loved for herself and not for whose daughter she was. Faith was grateful for her own comfortable obscurity.

"Thanks for listening again," Giselle said, standing.

"Anytime. But aren't you forgetting something?"

Giselle looked puzzled, then grinned. "Oh yeah. Something on military footwear during the Regency."

Faith got up too. "I think I have exactly what you need."

"Anyway, I'm glad they turn in their entries this morning. Then maybe everyone will relax and take some time to enjoy themselves."

The cat watched his human fill his dish with something she called "seafood blend," one of his favorites, and put fresh water in his bowl. He wasn't very interested in these "finalists" and "contests" she had been going on about all morning, and she hadn't said a word about that little white dog staying at the manor, so he turned his attention to his breakfast as she talked.

"Want to come with me?" she asked when he was almost finished.

He swallowed the last of his food and then came over to rub against her legs.

His human leaned down to give him a scratch behind his ears and under his chin. When she stood up straight, she picked up her purse, the purse she had been so finicky about when he had spilled it. "Come on."

The cat followed her through the garden and up to the manor and waited politely for her to open the door, just as if he didn't have his own ways in and out anytime he wanted.

"Come on," she said again when they got inside and were about halfway to the room with the books.

But he was more interested in the second floor. With admirable nonchalance, he wandered toward the staircase.

"Rumpy." His human stood there with her hands on her hips.

He didn't dignify that name with a response. Instead, he gave one irritated twitch of his stubby tail and walked deliberately up the stairs.

"Fine," she called after him. "I have work to do anyway. You behave." She had yet to realize that he always behaved. In one way or another.

Once the cat reached the second floor, he made his usual rounds, looking for any foolhardy mice that might have gotten in. There never were any, but that was no doubt due to his constant vigilance.

Afterward, he crept into the room where the dog was staying. Getting more than a glimpse of her had been harder than he'd thought. It seemed like one of the humans was always carrying her around. It was a wonder she could still walk under her own power.

Now, though, the room was empty. He investigated the wastepaper basket and a drawer that had been left open, but there was nothing intriguing in either one of them. He examined a few little bottles that had been left by the bathroom sink, found an earring, and enjoyed batting it around the floor for a few minutes. Then, realizing there wasn't much else to do here, he decided to see if he could figure out where the dog was now. She was probably having her toenails painted again. Why would she allow herself to suffer such indignity?

The cat was about to walk out when he heard the key in the door. In a flash he dived under the bed and crouched there, unmoving. Through the opening in the pale gold ruffle of fabric around the bottom of the bed, he watched one of the humans enter the room.

15

The human walked straight into the bathroom.

Curious, the cat crept out from under the bed and hid under the big chair that was long enough for humans to stretch their legs out on. It was closer to the bathroom and had a ruffle around it too. He could see perfectly now and still not be seen.

The human picked up one of the bottles that was sitting by the sink and emptied it on the counter. There were five or six small oblong things in it, almost like the beads his own human forbade him to carry off when he was at home—not that this ever stopped him. But these were red on one end and blue on the other with a white stripe around the middle, and they weren't hanging on a string. The human opened up one of them and shook out a white powder into the sink, then took out a different bottle, a tiny one, and opened it too.

The cat sniffed and then huffed, not wanting to breathe in any of whatever was in that tiny bottle. It didn't smell right, but most humans had such a poor sense of smell that he bet none of them would even notice.

The human glanced at the door, maybe trying to hear if anyone else was coming, and then put some of the stuff from the tiny bottle into the open red-and-blue thing. When that was closed up again, the human did the same with the rest of the oblong things and put them back into the bigger bottle, closed it up, and set it where it had been before. Stuffing the tiny bottle into a deep pocket, the human went to the door, opened it just a crack to peek into the hallway, and darted away.

The cat heard the click of the key in the lock, and then there was silence.

After a moment the cat leaped up on the counter by the sink. He sniffed the bottle. It definitely smelled different than it had before. Whatever had been put inside those little bead things was not at all nice.

He went out into the hall using one of his secret ways around the locked door. Unnoticed, he followed the human to another room, this one also empty. Inside, the human opened the closet door, took down the suitcase on the shelf at the top, and placed it on the bed. With the quick flick of a blade, the human cut a small hole in the suitcase lining and put the strange-smelling bottle inside. The suitcase looked empty again. In another minute, it was back in the top of the closet and the human was out the door, locking it afterward.

The cat came out from behind a big chair and trotted into the hallway. The human was almost as good at getting in and out of locked places as he was, but the cat couldn't figure out the point of all this. He knew that humans had some very odd habits, but this couldn't possibly be good.

Lunch that afternoon was a group affair. Ralph insisted that Faith join them in honor of all the help she had been during the week. She wouldn't have missed it for the world. Of course, she was interested in knowing what Ralph and Camilla might say about the entries they had received. But beyond that, what better way to get a look at all the suspects at the same time and see them interacting with Camilla? And what better way to keep an eye on Camilla so there wouldn't be any more incidents?

A little before the scheduled lunchtime, Faith stopped at the front desk to reassure Marlene for the hundredth time that she had made sure Camilla had everything she needed from the library. She had just turned toward the banquet hall when she heard Melanie and Tony coming down the stairs, their voices low and urgent. Were they arguing?

She started to let them know she was there when she made out what Melanie was saying.

". . . not cheating."

"I didn't say it was," Tony told her. "But I think it would be better if you said something. They'd understand. You wouldn't want anyone accusing—"

"Tony. Melanie," Faith said brightly, as if she hadn't overheard anything. "I'm glad I won't be the last one in the banquet hall."

"I understand you're having lunch with us again," Tony said with his usual charming smile.

Faith nodded. "Ralph invited me. With everyone leaving tomorrow, this will be one of our last chances to be together as a group. I've had a great time getting to know all of you and seeing how different writers work."

"You've been a lot of help," Melanie assured her. "I could use you around the house when I'm writing."

Faith laughed and went with them into the hall, but she didn't sit down until Camilla came in and chose a seat. Then Faith sat right next to her.

"I hope you don't mind," Faith said by way of excuse, "but I wanted to see how you're doing today. You seem to be getting around all right."

Camilla gave her a cheery smile and raised her bandaged wrist. "Oh, sure, honey. Like I said before, this isn't anything."

"What about your knee?"

"It's hardly even sore today."

"I told you she wouldn't stay cooped up for long," Giselle remarked from across the table.

"It's not much fun being at a fabulous place like this if all you do is sit in your room," Camilla insisted. "Emma and I had a very nice visit to the garden and the maze this morning. It did us a world of good."

The little dog looked up at Camilla from the chair on her other side, her button eyes full of pure adoration.

For once Giselle didn't make a face. In fact, she seemed more calm and confident than Faith had ever seen her.

"I guess it did me good to get out for a while too." Giselle glanced at Alex, who was seated next to her.

He gave her a quick wink.

Faith had to bite her lip to keep from grinning. So they'd had their talk.

"I finally had a chance to go into town and look around," Ann said. Faith could see there was a touch of healthy color in her face. "It was nice to get out and get some sun."

Melanie shook her head. "I couldn't stand being inside for a whole week, even if I did have a lot of work to do. I would never have gotten it done if I hadn't spent time out by the water."

"I know all of you have worked hard," Ralph said, "and it shows."

"It's been so interesting helping them research." Faith glanced around the table, seeing the same eagerness on everyone else's faces. None of them looked capable of hurting anyone. She faced Camilla. "I'm dying to know what you thought about the entries."

Camilla appeared startled. "Well, you know we can't—"

"I know you can't say anything specific yet," Faith interrupted. "But overall, what do you think?"

"They've made it *very* hard for us to settle on only one," Camilla said with a smile.

Ralph nodded. "We've each read the entries separately. After lunch, we'll get together and compare notes and eventually pick a winner. As Camilla said, it's going to be a tough job. All three of them are excellent. Oh, and Tony has a little reward for each of you for all the hard work you've put in this week. Tony?"

Tony produced three boxes, each elaborately wrapped, and handed them out. "Alex, you get the big one. Melanie and Ann, I think you'll be happy to get these."

Alex tore off the glitzy paper and opened his box. His eagerness turned to amusement. "This may be the greatest gift I've ever received." He pulled out both of his phones and then his tablet. "I've missed all of you."

"Oh, wow." Melanie immediately turned it on and checked her phone for messages. "It's going to take me hours just to return texts."

Ann simply put her phone in her purse. "I'd rather check my e-mail."

"You'll find the Wi-Fi is available now," Ralph said, "and all three of you have my thanks for being such good sports about this. You too, Faith." He lifted his coffee cup to her in a lighthearted toast.

A few minutes later lunch was served. As Wolfe and Faith had discussed with Brooke earlier in the day, there were no shared dishes. The tricolor salad was already topped with Gorgonzola blue cheese dressing. The stuffed chicken roulade lay on its bed of julienne carrots and zucchini smothered with bourbon mustard sauce. The herb-roasted new potatoes were merely seasoned, so there was nothing to be added there. For good measure, each plate was provided with tiny individual shakers of salt and pepper. If anyone made an attempt to doctor someone else's food this time, it should be fairly obvious.

Faith drew a deep breath before she ate her first bite. Brooke's meals not only looked amazing, but they smelled divine. The smoky aroma of tender chicken blended in perfect harmony with the more delicate scents of the vegetables and only a hint of the mustard's tang, and the taste lived up to its promise.

"Delicious," Camilla said. "I might have to steal this Brooke of yours and take her home with me."

"You're not home enough to keep a full-time cook," Giselle said, but for once her tone was more indulgent than annoyed. "But maybe Jenny could get some of her recipes."

Jenny flushed slightly. "I don't really do anything fancy. Just simple things if Camilla isn't going out."

"Don't you worry, honey." Camilla patted her assistant's arm. "I know I keep you hopping enough as it is. I won't expect you to do any gourmet cooking too."

"This is superb," Ann said with a nod at Ralph. "Win or lose, I've enjoyed the experience. Thank you."

"You're welcome," Ralph said. "All of you. Northanger Press has been happy to have you. And I'm serious. Each of your entries was excellent. It's a real shame there can be only one winner."

"There's always independent publishing, I guess," Alex offered, a forkful of salad halfway to his mouth.

"If you have the money to do it right. Though I don't suppose that would be a problem for all of us," Ann said, giving Melanie a pointed look.

Melanie smiled in return. "I want to be a writer, not a promoter and a cover designer and an editor and all that. Sure, there are people who do that and do very well at it, but not everybody is suited for it." Her expression turned a bit harder. "My family has a little money. I could buy my way into print, but I want to earn it. I'd rather win contests like these and get noticed for my writing and have contracts offered to me because my books are good, not because of my money or my family's connections. I want to make it on my own. Who wouldn't?"

Faith couldn't help noticing Tony's gaze on Melanie now, admiration and perhaps something a little softer shining in his expression. Maybe they had more in common than Faith had realized before.

Melanie's smile returned, this time rather mischievous as she turned to Camilla. "And on my own, I pretty much plan to take your place as the best-selling Regency romance writer in the country."

Camilla laughed. "You're certainly welcome to try. Competition only makes us both better. Still, all work and no play, right? I hope we'll all have a good time at the ball tonight and forget about work. One of you is definitely going to get a chance to give me a run for my money—or I should say Northanger's money—but not tonight."

"Are you sure you're up to going tonight?" Ann asked, gesturing at Camilla's bandaged wrist. "You must be pretty sore still."

"A little," Camilla admitted. "But it's nothing to worry about."

Ann nodded. "I suppose the hospital gave you some strong painkillers."

"They always give me the same thing, and I never take it." Camilla made a disdainful face. "It makes me too sleepy, and I don't want to sleep through the ball."

"I can understand that," Ann said. "Maybe there's something milder you could take."

"I have some extra-strength, rapid-release medication I always keep handy," Camilla replied. "It says it's a sleep aid too, but it never affects me that way. It's pretty good for pain. I'll take it if I need to tonight. I don't want to miss anything."

"You at least take that if you're hurting," Giselle said. "Promise me, okay?"

Camilla rolled her eyes in a perfect imitation of her daughter. "Yes, mother."

Everyone laughed, including Alex, but there was a gentle fondness in his laugh that might not have been there before this morning.

"You haven't had any other problems, have you?" Faith asked Camilla. "It seems like it's been fairly quiet today. I think having Giselle and Jenny with you is a good way to discourage any other possible incidents." She looked at the young women. "One of you has been with her all the time, right?"

"Pretty much," Giselle said. "We've been taking turns."

"I wish they could do something about the reporters calling, though," Camilla grumbled, buttering a yeast roll. "I imagine that little dear who waylaid me at the hospital must have told the world I was there. Now everybody wants an interview."

"Oh, Mom," Giselle said, "you probably don't want to look at the Internet right now."

"Why not?"

"Evidently you had a near-death experience and now you're hiding for your life somewhere in Cape Cod, stalked by a relentless killer."

Camilla shook her head. "Ridiculous. A couple of tiny episodes do not equal attempted murder."

"Have you had a lot of calls?" Faith asked.

"A few," Camilla admitted.

Jenny rubbed her forehead, looking pained. "I've been taking calls from reporters all morning, though Camilla did talk to some of them."

"I have a couple of friends in the news business," Camilla said. "I thought maybe I could get them to downplay it. Report the facts and get rid of the wild speculation."

"Any publicity is good publicity, right?" Ralph said with a wink. "Especially with your new book coming out."

Camilla laughed. "If you say so."

"We can have the front desk hold your calls if you'd like," Faith offered. "You're here to enjoy yourself, not be annoyed by the press."

Camilla waved her hand dismissively. "I don't have time to deal with them or any other foolishness. But I'm sure Jenny can handle the calls."

Jenny nodded. "I've been telling them the fall wasn't serious, you're recovering very well, and you don't have any further comment."

"Perfect," Camilla said, then turned to Ralph. "You and I still have a lot of work to do before the ball tonight, so we'd better eat our lunch and get back to it. We'll work in your room, so if there are more calls, we won't even hear the phone."

"Good enough," Ralph said. "The rest of you have earned some time off. Just don't be late for tonight's festivities, and don't be surprised if some of the fans want your autographs too. I mean, in case one of you becomes a huge success later on."

"I hope you all do," Camilla told the contestants. "I was so impressed by the entries. I don't see any reason why each of you couldn't do well with your books." She looked down at her plate and then around the table. "Goodness, here I've been chatting on, and the food's getting cold. Everybody, eat. It's going to be a big night."

When lunch was over, Camilla and Ralph went up to the Agatha Christie Suite to deliberate about who the grand prize winner would be. Ann excused herself to take a brief nap before preparing for the ball. Tony and Melanie invited everyone else to come down to the beach with them. When no one accepted, they rushed out. Faith guessed they departed quickly before anyone had second thoughts and decided to join them. Jenny took Emma out to the garden for a walk before heading to Camilla's room to handle any more telephone calls.

That left only Faith, Giselle, and Alex finishing their coffee.

The couple didn't seem to be in any hurry to leave the banquet hall, so Faith got to her feet. "I have work to do too. I'll see both of you later tonight."

Giselle glanced at Alex and then stood up. "Um, Alex and I are going bike riding, but in case we don't get back before the library is closed, would you mind if I come with you now? I'd like to get another one of those Campion books, if I could." She gave Alex a shy smile. "Meet you out there?"

"Sure thing, Gizi," Alex said, his eyes warm. "Don't be long."

"You're a fast reader," Faith said as she and Giselle walked through the lobby toward the library. "You already took four or five of the series, didn't you?"

There was a touch of color in Giselle's cheeks, and her eyes were very bright. "I just have to tell you about me and Alex before I explode."

"I thought you must have had a talk," Faith said with a knowing look.

Giselle nodded eagerly. "You were right. I told him I was sorry, and he doesn't hate me at all."

"I never believed he did."

Giselle's expression clouded. "I guess I hurt him more than I realized when I accused him like that and told him not to ever call. He admitted that he hasn't done anything since we broke up except work on his book and get ready for this contest, but when it was over, win or lose, he was going to try one more time to get in touch with me. I don't know if that means anything quite yet, but at least he and I can talk, right?"

Faith unlocked the library door. "And go to the ball tonight."

The sparkle came back into Giselle's eyes. "I can't wait till he sees me all dressed up. And won't he be wonderful dressed like Mr. Darcy?"

"I'm sure he'll be very dapper. But what does your mother think of him now?"

Giselle bit her lip. "I haven't exactly told her. She's been so busy trying to judge the contest, and with everything that's been happening to her, I didn't wish to add anything else." She glanced around, making sure there was no one else nearby. "I wanted to ask you if you know anything more about what's going on. You don't think somebody means to really hurt Mother, do you? It doesn't even make sense."

"We'll just have to make sure she's safe until you both return home."

"She says I should enjoy myself and not worry so much, and I guess she's right." Giselle sighed. "I do tend to blow things out of proportion sometimes."

"You are staying with her all the time, aren't you?" Faith asked.

"Me or Jenny, yeah. And she's with Ralph now, so that's okay, isn't it?"

Faith nodded, but she wasn't totally sure it was. She wasn't certain anyone could be trusted right now. "Okay, you'd better get your book and get going. Alex is waiting for you."

"Oh, I didn't want a book. Not really. I haven't made much progress on the ones I already have. I only wanted to tell you about Alex. And to thank you for your advice." With a wave, she scurried out of the library and out of sight.

Faith thought about how easy it would be for someone to cause more trouble during tonight's ball. If it was hard to keep Camilla safe when only a handful of people had access to her, what would it be like when the Great Hall Gallery was packed with her fans, all hoping for an autograph and a word with their beloved author?

It wouldn't hurt to call in some reinforcements.

16

"**H**appy birthday!" Faith said as soon as her aunt picked up the phone. "How are you?"

"Wonderful," Eileen said. "I had lunch with an old school friend I haven't seen in years, and then we went antiquing. But what are you calling me for? The ball's still on for tonight, isn't it? If I don't get to meet Camilla Courtenay, I may never forgive you."

"No, nothing as dire as that. But there has been a bit of trouble." Faith told Eileen about the recent incidents, sticking to the facts and adding none of her own unsupported suspicions. "There's really no way any of those things could have been accidents, but the police haven't found any evidence to show who might be behind them or why. We're only trying to make sure nothing else happens to Camilla while she's at the manor. That's why I thought I'd call you."

"What am I supposed to do? Subdue any dangerous criminals I happen to see lurking around?"

Faith laughed. "I just want you and Brooke and Midge to keep your eyes open during the ball, see if anything strange is going on. We probably won't end up spotting anything unusual. But it wouldn't hurt to be on alert in case our culprit plans to use the crowd to cover up some nefarious activities or has even hired somebody else to do the dirty work. What do you say?"

"It sounds like fun actually. And all I have to do is watch people? I'm definitely in."

"You have to watch people without looking like you're watching people. That's different than simply watching people."

"I see," Eileen said with a soft laugh. "Well, I think I'm up to the challenge."

As soon as she got off the phone, Faith called Midge, who was delighted to help with the surveillance.

Then Faith went to the kitchen. She was in the middle of telling Brooke her plan when Marlene walked in.

Much to Faith's surprise, Marlene was in favor of the idea. "I don't want anything else to happen to Ms. Courtenay during her stay, but I don't want the whole police force standing around. It doesn't look good for the manor."

"If something happened to Camilla," Faith said, "that wouldn't look very good either."

"That's why I think it's a great idea for the four of you to be on the lookout for mischief," Marlene said. "I'll be watching too."

"You're coming?" Brooke asked, clearly taken aback.

Marlene gave her a cold smile. "I hope that meets with your approval."

"Um, sure, but I didn't think you were going. For some reason," Brooke finished lamely.

"I will be there. Have you prepared the desserts? Mr. Carlson was extremely particular about everything being authentic."

"Yes," Brooke said, "all the sweets were made from genuine Regency recipes. We're having baked apples, Savoy biscuits, flummery, sugarplums, sherry trifle, queen cakes, and crumpets with lemon curd."

Marlene narrowed her eyes. "Flummery?"

"It's like blancmange, sort of a custard. I put it in a decorative nineteenth-century pineapple mold. I think it will be very pretty."

"See that it is," Marlene snapped. "Faith, I want you to get here before the ball begins. You and the rest of your club."

"We're already planning to," Faith assured her.

With a curt nod, Marlene marched out of the kitchen.

"I hope nothing happens tonight," Brooke said, finally exhaling completely. "Marlene would blame us somehow."

"I think I'll see if Wolfe wants to help too." Faith felt better just knowing he'd be in this with them.

"Do you think we should ask Ralph? He'd help, wouldn't he?"

Faith shook her head. "I don't want him to know we're watching. I don't want any of the contest-related people to know. Whoever's been doing these things is certainly one of them, and we need to figure out which one."

"But he's Camilla's editor," Brooke protested. "His publishing company has made tons of money off her. Why would he kill the goose that lays the golden egg?"

"It doesn't make much sense, does it? And to be honest, he seems like such a nice guy that I can't imagine he's the one. But they all seem very nice. None of them seems like the type to try to hurt or kill someone else, but appearances can be deceiving. Clearly one of these seemingly nice people is up to no good, and we can't rule any of them out quite yet."

Faith thought of Camilla. She was now in Ralph's room judging the contest entries. Surely even if he was the one, he wouldn't be so overconfident as to try to pull something else when he would be the only possible suspect.

"What?" Brooke asked her when she didn't say anything for a moment.

"Nothing. But I don't like how this whole thing is set up for tonight. I wish there was some way to keep the general public out. Just for Camilla's sake."

"That would sort of spoil the whole purpose of a fan event," Brooke pointed out.

"Yeah, I suppose it would," Faith admitted with a smile. "So what about tonight? I'm so glad you don't have to work. Are you bringing a date?" She knew someone as perky and cute as Brooke would have no trouble finding one.

"No way. Diva and Bling gave a definite thumbs-down to the guy

I went out with last." Brooke shrugged. "Besides, who knows who'll be at the ball tonight?" Her eyes sparkled with excitement. "I'm keeping my options open."

Faith took a critical look at herself in her floor-length mirror. It had taken her longer than she had planned to get her hair exactly right, but now it was furiously pinned into what she hoped was an effortless-looking bun at the back of her head. An exasperating battle with a small-barreled curling iron had finally achieved the desired ringlets all around her hairline, and the whole thing was finished off with a band of ivory silk that matched her dress.

She had fallen in love with the pattern at the local sewing center, and a seamstress had made the dress for her. It had been a little pricey for one night, but it fit exquisitely and she felt like a princess in it. The ivory silk was dotted with flecks of dark gold, and elegant dark gold vines were embroidered on the bottom eighteen inches of the skirt that gave no more than a glimpse of her ivory satin slippers. The empire waist, puffed sleeves, and swooping neckline were period perfection, and when she draped a delicate silk shawl around her shoulders and picked up an ivory fan, she felt as if there must be a barouche outside the cottage door, waiting to whisk her away to Almack's to be the darling of the haut ton.

Watson sat on her bed, looking as if he wasn't quite sure what she was thinking by dressing as she had.

She laughed. "You're always in formal wear, so you shouldn't be surprised if I want to dress up sometimes too."

With a huff, he leaped off the bed and headed to the front door, glancing back at her expectantly.

"All right, all right, you can come too," Faith said as she followed him. She retrieved the cheerfully wrapped package that lay on the sofa. "But no shenanigans, understand?"

Watson appeared to ignore that particular recommendation. As soon as she opened the door, he was off like a shot into the garden twilight.

17

The ball wouldn't officially begin for another half hour, but the Great Hall Gallery was already filling up fast. Faith spotted Brooke and Midge, both lovely in their Regency gowns and hairstyles, and went over to them.

"Oh, you two look fabulous." She touched the puffed sleeve of Midge's gown. "So pretty. You look positively royal, Midge. And I love that cerulean on you, Brooke. And your hair! I didn't know how you would manage since you keep yours short. It's so cute."

Brooke patted her blonde locks, now in a riot of Grecian ringlets and banded in the same blue as her dress. "I'm glad I didn't have to wear a wig."

"It's perfect," Faith assured her, then turned to Midge. "And so is yours. Very period."

Midge's shoulder-length hair was parted in the middle, combed straight and smooth to right above her ears and then hanging in thick curls from there. Her Pomona-green silk gown was trimmed with pale yellow lace that echoed the tiny yellow flowers she had pinned above one ear.

Midge grinned. "I don't know how he could, but Peter loves it. Of course, I nearly swooned when I saw him dressed up. It took more than a little coaxing to get him into that outfit, but it was worth it. He'll be back in a few minutes, and you can see for yourself."

Faith scanned the gallery, clutching her package a little closer. "You haven't seen Eileen, have you?"

"Not yet." Brooke gestured to the package. "Is that what I think it is?"

Faith nodded. "I took care of everything earlier today. I hope the birthday girl likes them."

"I'm sure she will," Eileen said, coming up behind them.

Despite her warm smile, Faith's aunt looked rather formidable in a plum gown of watered silk and a lavender turban that sported a large opal and a single ostrich feather. She had on the most gloriously ostentatious paste diamonds Faith had ever seen. A silk shawl that matched the turban was draped over her arm.

"Look at you." Faith could hardly keep from laughing because her aunt's outfit was so flawless. "Lady Catherine de Bourgh would be absolutely green with envy if you showed up at Rosings Park dressed like that."

Eileen gave her a serene smile and a slight nod and then laughed. "Might as well do it up right, don't you think?"

"Speaking of done right . . . ," Brooke murmured, her gaze focused toward the lobby.

Faith turned to see Wolfe, perfection itself from his polished Hessian boots to his exquisitely tied cravat, approaching them.

"Good evening, ladies." He made a graceful bow and then peered at them through his quizzing glass. "May I say you are all ravishing this evening?"

"Impertinence," Eileen said as haughtily as a duchess.

Brooke giggled behind her fan. "Oh, sir!"

"Thank you," Midge said demurely.

Wolfe smiled and turned to Faith.

She lowered her head modestly and curtsied. When she looked up, she met his eyes.

Wolfe held her gaze just long enough that she began to feel the heat of a blush in her face, and then he looked over the whole group once more. "I don't know how you ladies expect to inconspicuously observe our suspects when no one will be able to take their eyes off you."

"Nonsense," Eileen assured him. "Have you seen the people who are already here? No one will notice us in the least."

"We do have an interesting variety of guests, don't we?" Wolfe said. Faith glanced around the room. Most of the people had on reasonable facsimiles of Regency wear, many of the ladies in white muslin, the gentlemen in black cutaway coats with tails, satin waistcoats, and high starched cravats. But some of the others had dressed more as if they were from the American Civil War, King Arthur's court, or some nebulous period in between. Nonetheless, they were a colorful gathering, and they all looked delighted to dress as their fictional heroes and heroines and see their literary idol, the great Camilla Courtenay.

Midge's husband, Peter, joined the group and tipped his top hat. He looked like he'd just stepped off the set of a big-budget Jane Austen film. "Good evening," he said with a smile.

The others greeted him warmly.

"I can't wait to find out who the winner is," Faith said. "I don't know how they could possibly choose between the three of them."

Eileen clicked her tongue. "Don't think you're going to get me off track at this point, young lady. As the only birthday girl here, I have the right to know what's in that package."

Faith held the gift behind her back. "All in good time. I was going to lock it in the library until later on."

"Where's the fun in that?"

"I guess I could give it to you now and then lock it up, so you don't have to carry it around all night."

"That sounds good," Eileen said brightly.

"I don't know." Faith bit her lip, pretending to be undecided. "Maybe you won't like it."

"I'll love it." Eileen held out both hands.

With a grin, Faith gave it to her. "Happy birthday."

Eileen ripped the wrapping paper off, and her face lit up. "So that's where my copy of *A Love Abandoned* got to." She flipped open the cover and gasped at the newly written autograph. "I always wanted to have it signed. And what's this?" She regarded the new book that accompanied it. "The twenty-fifth-anniversary edition. Oh, it's wonderful!"

"The cover's not nearly as cheesy as the one on the first edition," Brooke observed.

Faith agreed. The designer of the new cover had eschewed the look of the first edition—the windblown heroine in a low-cut gown, swooning in the muscular hero's arms—favoring instead a single rose, a delicate lace glove, and a torn wedding invitation. It was gorgeous, evocative, and ideal for the story.

"Nice," Wolfe said, smiling at Faith.

"You got Camilla to sign this one too!" Eileen exclaimed, peering inside the cover. "This may be the best present ever." She gave her niece a tight hug and a kiss on the cheek. "Do you think I'll get to meet her tonight?"

"I'll make sure of it," Faith promised. "Now you'd better give those back to me. You're the only person who has the anniversary edition until it's officially released later on tonight, and I don't want anyone else to see it and cause a stampede."

Eileen clutched the books to her heart and then, with obvious reluctance, handed them over.

"Don't worry," Faith said. "They'll be safe in the library. Now, I need to hurry and put them away before Ralph gets everything started. Be sure to keep an eye on everyone here."

"I haven't seen any of your suspects yet," Midge said. "But I don't think I'd even know who they are."

"I'll point them out," Wolfe offered. "They should arrive any moment now."

Faith found Tony standing anxiously by the library's locked door. He was always easy on the eyes, but he looked especially nice dressed as a Regency gentleman.

"Camilla is going to make you sit for a photo session if she sees you in that outfit," she told him, smiling.

He sighed. "Now you know I couldn't do that. Someone back in England would no doubt tell my aunt, and she'd have me tracked down quicker than you can say 'no more allowance.'"

"I suppose that wouldn't work at all. You should think of some excuse if it comes to that, because Ralph doesn't seem the type to deny Camilla very much."

"I'll work on it. For now, Ralph sent me to ask you a favor. Would it be all right with you if Camilla and the finalists wait in the library until Ralph makes the introductions? If Camilla is standing out in the gallery, everyone there will recognize her and want autographs. She's more than happy to do autographs but only after the important business is seen to. Would that work?"

"Of course. Let me put this package in here, and we'll go up and get everyone. They're still in their rooms, right?"

"Actually, they're all in Ralph's room, waiting to see what we should do. Thank you."

Faith managed to get everyone into the library without incident. The contestants were all impeccably dressed. Camilla had provided beautiful gowns for Jenny and Giselle, and Emma had a tiny faux diamond tiara perched on her head. Or maybe, considering Camilla's attachment to the little dog, they were real diamonds. Faith wouldn't have been surprised if they were.

Camilla was dressed in gold satin with seed pearls, and she wore rubies at her throat and ears. Her white hair was piled atop her head, no doubt augmented with a hairpiece, and crowned with gold-and-ruby ribbons and half a dozen ostrich feathers. Her small feet were ensconced in gold satin slippers laced with ruby ribbons. The bandage on her wrist was neatly concealed by an exquisite pair of antique lace gloves. She might not have been tall or slender, but she made quite an impressive sight in full costume.

"Now," Ralph said, "you three stay in here with Camilla until I introduce you. Then we'll debut the new edition of *A Love Abandoned*. Everybody with a ticket gets a free copy." He patted his coat pocket. "Then we'll announce our new Northanger author. After that, Camilla will sign autographs and everyone will dance and mingle."

"Sounds great to me," Alex said, looking significantly at Giselle.

Camilla appeared concerned.

Ralph glanced at his watch. "It's about time to begin. I'm going to make sure everything's set to go. Tony will see to anything you might need until I get back."

Once he was gone, the rest of the group sat down before the library fireplace, careful of their finery. They all seemed a little tense.

"It's a big night," Tony said smoothly, "but I hope you'll relax and enjoy it. I know from talking with Ralph a bit ago that Northanger is really impressed with all the entries, so the three of you have a lot to be proud of."

"But only one of us will win." Melanie twisted the single long curl that fell down the side of her neck, threatening to unsettle the large knot of hair pinned above it.

"True," Tony admitted, "but maybe the week hasn't been a complete waste."

Melanie colored faintly at that comment.

"We each got a nice trip to Cape Cod, all expenses paid, and a chance to have our writing seen by a major publisher," Ann said, drawing her fringed shawl more tightly around herself. "And a chance to dress up. That last part isn't exactly my cup of tea, but I guess it isn't too bad."

"It can't hurt to be able to tell other publishers we each won our regional contests," Alex added, and then he squeezed Giselle's hand. "There are also less obvious benefits."

Camilla narrowed her eyes. "We'll be going back home tomorrow, Giselle. Don't forget."

Giselle nodded, looking as if she had been caught coming in after curfew.

"It's going to be a lovely evening, I'm sure." Camilla smiled coolly at Alex. "Let's all remember why we're here and not complicate things, shall we?"

"Of course, ma'am," he said, spreading one white-gloved hand over his frilled shirt and bowing his head in finest Regency form. "But after tonight, we're all at liberty to live as we please." He turned to Giselle. "Are we not?"

She wilted slightly under her mother's stern gaze, but then, her mouth tightening, she nodded.

Camilla turned to Faith, anxiety in her expression.

"I think you're right," Faith said to her. "Tonight is all about the contest and the fans who have come to meet you. You can see to anything else afterward."

Ralph reentered the library. "Are we ready?"

Everyone stood, smoothing skirts, lapels, and hair.

"There's a microphone set up near the string quartet," Ralph said. "Camilla and our contestants are to go directly over there. I'm going to talk about Northanger Press and explain the contest. After that, I'll introduce the finalists. When I call your name," he told the three, "be sure you nod and smile or wave or something to let the fans know who you are. Then I'll introduce Camilla."

Camilla made a quaint little curtsy.

"Camilla's going to say something about how she started in publishing," Ralph said, "and how she came to write *A Love Abandoned*. Then she'll reveal the new edition of the book and inform the guests that everyone with a ticket will get a free copy. I'll take back the mic and tell everyone that we want to declare the winner of the contest before we begin the ball. I'll hand you the envelope, Camilla, and you'll open it and announce our choice. Okay?"

Camilla nodded, a gleam of excitement in her eyes.

"The winner will have a chance to say a few words." Ralph glanced at each of the contestants. "Have all of you planned something to say?"

Ann nodded solemnly.

Melanie grinned. "I'll think of something."

"I have some stuff written down," Alex said, pulling a few ragged strips of paper out of his pocket as the group walked toward the library door. "I made a few notes so I wouldn't draw a blank at the last minute." He frowned, trying to arrange them into some semblance of order, and dropped several of them.

The others stopped to help him pick up the scraps.

But Camilla stood back, clutching the peacock feather fan that hung from a delicate golden cord around her wrist. "You don't actually mean to read something, do you?"

Alex looked up from where he knelt, obviously flustered and annoyed. "No, I don't mean to read something. They're just notes I made for myself."

"Come on," Ralph said, opening the door. "The quartet has already started playing."

"Wait." Giselle scooped up one more stray piece of paper and handed it to Alex. "You missed one."

Alex gave her a warm, grateful smile and stuffed the papers back into his pocket.

Camilla pursed her lips but said nothing.

"Ready?" Ralph urged. "Tony, please lead the way."

Tony walked out, trailed by Ralph with Camilla on his arm, the three finalists, Giselle, and Jenny, who was carrying a serene and regal Emma on her purple velvet pillow.

As soon as they left the library, Faith followed and locked the door behind her. Before she had a chance to take more than half a dozen steps, Marlene stopped her.

Marlene wore a gorgeous buttercup-yellow gown with cream-colored stripes, and her slippers, jewelry, and accessories set it off beautifully. "Everything in order?" she asked.

"Yes, everything's all set," Faith told her.

"Good. I'll be over at the signing table. Ms. Courtenay will come there after the winner is announced." Marlene lowered her voice. "Keep your eyes open."

Faith nodded and went to join her friends.

"Time for the big announcement," she whispered to Wolfe as Ralph halted the string quartet and stepped up to the microphone.

As Ralph had planned, he began talking about Northanger Press and its mission to find and publish only the very best authors.

He had spoken for only a minute or two when Faith noticed Jenny whispering something to Giselle. Then Jenny handed Emma to her and hurried around to the back of the crowd and out of the gallery.

By the time Camilla made her speech and the fans were applauding the twenty-fifth-anniversary edition of *A Love Abandoned*, Jenny was again standing beside Giselle. Something about Camilla's assistant seemed a little off, and she didn't immediately take charge of the dog. That wasn't like her.

Once the applause for Camilla died down, Ralph took the microphone from the author. "Now we come to the big reveal. Which of our three finalists has won the grand prize?" He pulled the envelope from his pocket and waved it dramatically in front of the audience. "Which one of these extremely talented writers has won a three-book publishing contract with Northanger Press and a worldwide publicity tour? Are you all ready to find out?"

The crowd clapped and cheered.

Camilla leaned into the mic. "Are you sure?"

The clapping and cheering grew louder.

With a grin, Ralph handed the envelope to Camilla.

There was sudden, eager silence in the gallery.

As everyone watched with bated breath, Camilla broke the seal of the envelope and removed the paper with a crisp rattle.

In spite of herself, Faith's pulse quickened.

Camilla scanned the paper, then glanced back at the finalists. Finally, she gave her audience a brilliant smile. "On behalf of Northanger Press, it's my pleasure to announce that our winner is—"

Someone screamed.

Faith looked around and saw Jenny sinking to her knees. Giselle tried to support her, but with Emma clutched in one arm, she couldn't keep her from falling to the floor. Jenny convulsed and gasped for breath.

"Jenny!" Camilla dropped the paper and the microphone, which hit the floor with a thud and a squeal of feedback. "What is it?" She ran to Jenny's side, watching her fighting for breath. "What's wrong?"

Ralph scrambled for the mic. "Is there a doctor here? A nurse? Anyone with medical training?"

"I'm calling 911," Wolfe said, already putting his phone to his ear.

"I'll see if I can help until the EMTs get here," Midge said, rushing to the front as Ralph continued to plead for assistance.

"Try to keep everyone calm," Faith told Brooke and Eileen. "I'll go with her."

The crowd murmured, and Tony did his best to keep the curious and intrusive attendees away from Jenny. Alex, Melanie, and Ann looked on anxiously. Giselle seemed stunned. Her mother sat on the floor next to Jenny, clutching her bewildered little dog in her arms. Tears streamed down Camilla's face.

Jenny was still now, her skin unnaturally pink.

"Do something," Camilla sobbed when Faith and Midge knelt at Jenny's side. "Please."

Faith patted her shoulder. "Wolfe called for an ambulance. Someone will be here soon. It'll be all right."

Midge pressed two fingers to Jenny's wrist and then to the side of her neck. She shook her head and exhaled heavily. "She's dead."

18

Faith could hardly believe she had heard Midge correctly, but it was true. Jenny was lying there on the gallery floor, unmoving in her demure white gown, her face covered with Eileen's pale shawl.

The contestants merely stood by, stunned and silent. Camilla had her face buried in Emma's white fur, sobbing painfully. Giselle sat on the floor beside her mother, one arm around her shaking shoulders, tears pooling in her eyes.

Wolfe immediately made an announcement to the guests, telling them that there had been a medical emergency and the rest of the evening's events were canceled. As Marlene herded them into the lobby and tried to answer with professional equanimity any complaints about not getting their promised autographs and free books, Wolfe lifted Jenny's slight body into his arms and carried it to the library.

"At least there will be a little more privacy in here," he said as Faith unlocked the door.

The rest of the Northanger group followed them inside and stood solemnly, almost dazed, as Wolfe gently placed the body on the sofa. No one spoke. No one knew what to say.

When the medical technicians arrived, there wasn't much for them to do but declare the young woman dead and take her body away. They said they couldn't give a cause of death until the coroner had had a chance to examine the body. They tried to get some information about Jenny from Camilla, who knew her best, but she was too distraught to be of any help. Giselle offered what she knew about Jenny and promised to have her mother fill in the rest when she was able. More quickly than Faith would have thought possible, they were gone. Jenny was gone.

Eileen, Brooke, and Midge quietly entered the library, looking toward Camilla with sympathy.

"Poor thing," Eileen said, her voice low. "Is there anything we can do to help?"

"I don't think so. I'm sorry this happened on your birthday." Faith gave her aunt the two autographed books that were her present. "Why don't you go home and get a good night's sleep, and we'll talk in the morning."

Eileen kissed her cheek and squeezed her arm. "Be sure to get some rest too. You call me tomorrow."

Faith nodded. "I'll be going home as soon as I see to things here."

"Peter's waiting in the lobby," Midge said, then pressed her lips together. "I'd be very interested in knowing what the cause of death was."

Brooke blinked at her. "You don't think—?"

Midge shushed her with a look. "Let's wait and see what the coroner has to say."

Brooke, Midge, and Eileen briefly told Wolfe good night and then slipped out of the library.

"Maybe I should take Mother upstairs and get her to lie down," Giselle suggested, breaking the silence that followed. "I guess we'll all do better for a night's rest."

"Sure," Ralph said. "That's a good idea."

"Before you go, Giselle," Faith said, "I have to ask you what Jenny said to you."

"What do you mean? She didn't say anything. She was standing there gasping and looking odd, and then she fell to the floor."

"No, before that. Was she feeling sick or something? She handed the dog to you and left the gallery for a few minutes. What did she say?"

"Oh." Giselle frowned, thinking. "Nothing really. She asked me to hold Emma and said she'd be right back. It wasn't anything."

"Jenny was all right before that?" Faith persisted.

"Yes, as far as I know," Giselle answered.

"She couldn't have had an allergic reaction?"

"I don't think so. I never heard she was allergic to anything, and she said she hadn't eaten anything since lunch. Wouldn't an allergic reaction have shown up way before now?"

"Jenny told me that everything going on tonight was giving her a headache." There was a worried wrinkle in Tony's forehead. "At the time I didn't think anything of it. I sure didn't think she was really sick."

"Obviously, I'm not a doctor or anything," Faith said, "but I'm not so sure whatever happened to her was a medical problem. Yes, people can die without warning from a sudden aneurysm, but I don't believe it usually causes those kinds of symptoms."

Camilla jerked her head up, not seeming to notice when Emma wriggled off her lap and went to Giselle. "What are you saying?" she asked, her voice thick with tears. "What do you mean?"

"Camilla," Ralph said soothingly, "nobody said—"

"If it wasn't natural causes, then it was murder. There are no other choices. Oh no!" Camilla wailed. "Why did this have to happen?"

"We don't know what happened yet," Ralph said soothingly.

"Oh yes we do. It's all my fault." Camilla buried her face in her hands, and one of the feathers from her hair drifted lazily to the floor. "All my fault."

"Of course it's not," Giselle said, picking up Emma. "Mother, how can it be?"

Camilla shook her head, apparently too choked up to speak.

Faith gave Camilla a moment and then touched her arm. "Please tell us. How can this be your fault?"

"Just leave me alone." Camilla ran her hands through her hair and flung the rest of the feathers and ribbons aside. She ran out of the room.

Ralph started after her.

Giselle stopped him. "Better let her cry it out." She collected her mother's abandoned fan and the tangle of ribbons and feathers from her hair. "I know she's not making sense right now, but there's no use trying to get her to talk until she's ready."

"Somebody should go with her," Ralph insisted.

Faith nodded. Somebody had to. "I'll make sure she's okay." She left the room and rushed through the gallery and the lobby.

Marlene caught her at the foot of the stairs. "What is going on? Ms. Courtenay—"

"Yes, I know. I think Jenny may have been poisoned. You should call the police, especially with everything else that's happened this week."

Marlene's expression turned grim. "Keep an eye on Ms. Courtenay until I can get Chief Garris back out here. If someone's after her, it's even more serious now."

Faith got to Camilla's room as quickly as she could. She started to knock, but the door wasn't locked. It wasn't even closed. It was only pushed to. She opened it a few inches and peered into the room. "Camilla?"

Camilla lay on the brocade chaise longue, her silk slippers kicked to the side, a washcloth over her face. She didn't respond.

"Camilla, it's Faith. May I come in?"

"Go away." Camilla's voice was little more than a whisper.

Faith came in anyway. "I only wanted to make sure you're all right."

"Of course I'm not all right." Camilla sat up and threw the washcloth onto the floor, her eyes red and fierce. "Jenny's dead."

"I know. But you—"

"She wouldn't be dead if it wasn't for me. Don't you understand? She wouldn't be dead if I hadn't brought her here and if someone wasn't trying to kill me. It's all my fault." Camilla wiped her eyes with the back of her hand, leaving a smear of blue eye shadow on the side of her face. "I should never have come."

Faith sat on the chaise beside Camilla and put one arm around her. "We're going to find out what happened, okay? Whoever did this will be brought to justice."

Camilla hid her face, her sobs making her body jerk.

"I need your help, though," Faith said gently. "Tell me what you remember Jenny doing this afternoon and evening. Did she eat anything? Drink anything? Did she take anything from anyone else?"

Camilla shook her head. "After we had lunch, she helped me get everything ready for tonight, my dress and all the things that went with it. She brushed Emma and got out her little tiara. Ralph came by to talk to me about the contest again, and we made our final selection."

"Was Jenny in here then?"

"She was sorting through my clothes, making sure everything I brought was ready to be packed up so we could leave tomorrow morning."

"And she was here the whole time? In your sight?"

"Except for about three minutes when I went to the bathroom," Camilla said, "but Ralph was still here, and he would have known if anyone else came into the room. Jenny didn't leave until it was time for her to get dressed for the ball. We all thought it was best if she got dressed while Giselle was helping me with my gown, and then when she came back, Giselle got dressed too."

"How long was Jenny gone?" Faith asked.

"I don't think it was even half an hour." Camilla gave her a teary smile. "You saw how she was. Jenny never bothered too much with fixing up, bless her heart, but I know she was fine then. And she was never out of my sight after that. Not until she—" She broke off with another torrent of sobs.

Faith wished there was something more she could do to comfort her. Maybe she should have brought Giselle with her. "It's all right. We'll figure this out. Jenny didn't mention talking to anyone when she went to get dressed?"

Camilla shook her head. "She didn't say anything. She never said much. Now poor Emma—oh." Obviously, she had just remembered she didn't have her dog with her.

"Don't worry, Mom. I've got her."

Faith turned toward the door. She hadn't heard Giselle come into the room.

Giselle walked over and handed the dog to her mother.

Camilla seemed relieved and grateful to have Emma in her lap again, and she hugged the dog close. Emma seemed to sense that now was not the time to be rambunctious, and she snuggled up to her mistress and held still.

"Maybe I'd better let your mother get some sleep," Faith said, standing. "Are you sure you don't remember Jenny saying anything else?"

"I'm sorry." Giselle glanced toward her mother and lowered her voice slightly. "She didn't tell me where she went or what she did. If she had a headache, I assume she came up to her room and took something for it. I don't know how someone could have given her poison, if that's really what happened. I hope this will turn out to be an accident or some kind of medical problem."

"I hope that's how it'll turn out too." Faith went to the door. "But maybe it'd be best if you stay with your mother tonight in case she needs you."

"I will." Giselle's smile was wry. "She'll never get out of that silly dress without help anyway."

Faith headed down the stairs to the lobby. She wasn't sure if everyone was still gathered in the library, but she hadn't locked up before she went to Camilla's room. She decided she'd better see to that.

Ralph, Tony, Wolfe, and the three contestants were waiting for her.

"Did you ever let them know who won?" Faith asked after she told them how Camilla was doing. "I suppose nobody thought of it with everything else that's happened."

"I thought of it," Melanie admitted, "but I didn't think it would be a good time to ask."

"I picked up the paper with the winner's name on it after Camilla dropped it," Ralph said. "It would be a little awkward to make the announcement now. I believe we ought to wait a couple of weeks and then maybe reveal the winner. Anything else would look pretty callous."

"Yes, it would," Faith said. "Have we heard from Chief Garris yet? Marlene was going to call."

Wolfe nodded gravely. "He's on his way. The coroner told him the preliminary tests on the body show the cause of death was cyanide poisoning."

19

Police Chief Andy Garris arrived at Castleton Manor, bringing with him Officers Mick Tobin and Bryan Laddy along with a warrant to search Jenny's room.

"I want you to understand that we're just gathering information," he told the group in the library once the official search was done. "No one is under arrest, and none of you has to talk to us if you don't want to. If I can rule any of you out as suspects, that'll make it easier for me to figure out who might be responsible. You're free to leave if you want to, but I have to get some facts so we'll know where to go from here."

The three police officers interviewed the witnesses separately, asking them to give their versions of the events leading up to Jenny's death, and then they examined the Great Hall Gallery. Finally, the entire group went back upstairs to do a preliminary search of the other guest rooms.

"Again," Chief Garris told them all when they stood at the door to Melanie's suite, "I don't have a warrant, and I'm not allowed to enter your rooms unless you agree to let me. I can't get a warrant without probable cause, and at this point I don't have enough evidence for that."

"You have the manor's full cooperation," Wolfe said, "as long as everyone is willing to let you in."

Alex narrowed his eyes. "I suppose the minute one of us objects, you'll decide he's the guilty party. Fine, search. I have nothing to hide."

Before anyone had a chance to say more, Camilla appeared, her ball gown discarded in favor of a pink flannel wrapper. She had Emma clutched in her arms, and Giselle was right behind her. "What is it? What's going on?"

"We're going to have a look at the rooms," Garris explained. "Nothing you need to worry about."

"You have to find out who did this," Camilla insisted. "Nobody would have wanted to kill Jenny. There wasn't any reason. Somebody was trying to get to me. I'm sure of it."

"Mother, you don't know," Giselle said. "If someone wanted to hurt you, they'd have poisoned you, not Jenny."

"I don't know." Camilla's voice was almost a sob. "But I'm sure she never did anybody any harm and no one could possibly have meant to hurt her."

There was a sudden commotion downstairs. Who in the world would that be in the middle of the night?

"See what that's about," the chief told Laddy.

"Right." The officer jogged downstairs.

Garris turned to Camilla. "We're doing our best. The more information we can gather, the sooner we'll figure it out. Now, Miss Wilde, if you'll let us, we'd like to have a look around your room."

Melanie glanced at Tony before nodding and unlocking her door.

Apart from a few pieces of clothing draped over the furniture, the room was neat and almost impersonal. There was a double frame on the bedside table, one side holding the picture of a green-eyed tabby cat and the other a photo of a middle-aged couple. The woman was an older, dark-haired version of Melanie. The man had thick blond hair and an easy smile. They were both dressed stylishly, tastefully, and expensively.

"Your parents?" Garris asked.

Melanie nodded.

Before he could ask another question, Laddy burst into the room. "It's reporters, Chief. Three of them demanding to talk to Ms. Courtenay."

Garris scowled. "Did you tell them to clear out?"

"They're not breaking the law by asking to speak to one of the guests."

"Do you want to see them, Ms. Courtenay?" the chief asked.

Camilla shook her head. "I just want them to leave me alone. Can't they leave me alone even for the night?"

"I'll see to them," Wolfe said, giving her a sympathetic look. "News like this always gets out, but I don't know how they found out so fast. I'll be back in a minute."

When he was gone, Faith noticed that Watson was sitting nonchalantly by the door. Wolfe must have let him in, though she hadn't seen it. She gave him a stern look. Now was not the time for him to start teasing Camilla's dog.

Fortunately, Watson stayed where he was, unnoticed. He simply watched as the police briefly searched Melanie's things. The reticule she had carried to the ball contained only her room key and her wallet. The room was clean. Nothing out of the ordinary.

"I suppose we can move on," Garris said, "unless there's something—"

"Chief?" Officer Tobin emerged from the bathroom carrying a little fabric-covered box containing a few pieces of costume jewelry. "You might want to see this." He poked around with one gloved finger, moving the jewelry out of the way until he found the object of his search. It was a pair of little eye screws, exactly like the ones that had held the trip wire in front of Camilla's door.

"You usually keep hardware in with your jewelry, Miss Wilde?" Garris asked.

Melanie gathered up her silk skirt and hurried over to him. "Those eye screws aren't mine. I only keep jewelry in there and nothing but the cheap stuff."

The chief nodded understandingly. "How do you suppose they got in there? Has anyone been in your room?"

Melanie shrugged, glancing nervously at everyone else. "Only the housekeepers, I suppose. I haven't invited anyone in. Why would someone put them in there?"

Faith looked into the box and then at the chief. "That's the same kind that was used on the trip wire, isn't it?"

"I'm assuming it's the same," he said. "We'll have to check to be sure."

"Nothing else here, Chief," Tobin announced.

"Okay. Bag those screws and put them in evidence."

"Wait a minute," Melanie said. "You don't think I—?"

"We don't think anything yet," Garris interrupted. "We're just having a look."

Melanie didn't respond, but when she saw Tony staring at her, she ducked her head.

Wolfe caught up to them as they all filed into Alex's room. "I took the reporters' cards and told them Ms. Courtenay would be in touch if she was interested in talking to them."

"Oh no," Camilla said, hugging Emma more closely. "I don't want to talk to anyone. Ever."

Wolfe gave her a comforting smile. "I'll throw them away then."

Alex stood right inside the door, back straight, head high, eyes defiant, as he watched his room being searched. In his black coat and starched cravat, he looked like a pink of the ton who'd been accused of cheating at cards at his club and was waiting for a retraction.

Watson, looking every bit as well-dressed, padded in and sat silently behind him, observing everyone and everything. For once, he didn't seem interested in the little dog. What was he up to?

In a surprisingly short time, the officers went through the jumble of papers and the clothes and toiletries Alex had brought with him.

"Nothing here, Chief," Laddy said. "Should we go over it all again?"

"What else do you need from me?" Alex demanded. "Do you want me to turn out my pockets now?"

Garris shook his head. "Mr. Denning was good enough to let us have a look. There's nothing here that would show probable cause."

Alex emptied his pockets anyway, pulling out a key ring, a wallet, and the paper scraps he had dropped before.

"What are those?" the chief asked, pointing at the scraps.

Alex gave him the papers. "Notes for a speech. Go ahead and read them. I don't need them anymore."

The police chief shuffled through them.

Faith didn't know how anyone could make sense of the notes written on strips torn off a variety of papers, but evidently Alex was comfortable with them. She noticed each one had a circled number in one corner. Maybe that was how he kept them in order. Still, it seemed . . .

Garris frowned at one of the slips. It was torn, just as the others were, but it wasn't written on or numbered. "What's this one?"

Alex took it, glanced at both sides, and gave it back to him. "I don't know. A receipt. Maybe it was already in the suit before I rented it. Is it from the costume shop?"

"It's from the airport."

Faith studied the receipt over the chief's shoulder. It was definitely from the airport on the day Alex and the others had come to the manor. It showed the time and the date and was torn right where it listed what had been purchased. *5 BAG P*. That was all. She was sure it would fit nicely with the receipt Watson had been playing with a few days ago.

"It's the rest of the receipt for the peanuts," she said.

"Did you buy peanuts at the airport, Mr. Denning?" Garris asked.

"No. I told you already that I didn't. I don't know how that receipt got in my pocket. I dropped my notes earlier tonight. Everyone saw it, and everyone helped me pick them up." Alex regarded everyone standing there. "Anybody could have handed me that." He glanced at Giselle, appearing uncertain.

Faith remembered that Giselle had been the one to give Alex the last bit of paper, the one she said he had missed. *Oh, surely not.*

The chief looked at Alex speculatively, saying nothing.

"What kind of idiot would I be to keep a receipt like that after the rest of it had already been found?" Alex said. "And in my pocket? Really?"

Giselle moved closer to her mother, hurt and wariness now in her eyes. "You wouldn't have done something like that. Alex, you couldn't have."

"No, I wouldn't, and I didn't," he said tightly, "but maybe someone wants everyone to think I did."

"Let's save the discussion until after we've finished looking around," Garris said, putting the scrap into one of his little plastic bags and giving it to Laddy. "Fair enough?"

There were no objections, and they proceeded to Ann's room. Apart from a book about the prince regent and another on nineteenth-century carriages that were sitting on the overstuffed chair in front of the windows, the room was exactly the way housekeeping had left it before her arrival. It appeared she had come to Castleton Manor focused on nothing but the contest.

Faith noticed that Watson was still staying with the group. This time he was sitting neatly underneath the bedside table. He watched as the officers swiftly and professionally searched everything.

Finally, the chief turned to the closet. He patted down the clothes hanging there, then took the suitcase from the shelf and set it on the bed. "Is this locked?"

Ann shook her head. "There's nothing in it, but feel free to look."

He opened the case and shrugged. "Like you said."

Before Garris could close it again, Watson jumped onto the bed and peered inside. That made Emma start barking.

"Watson," Faith scolded, "get off there."

He ignored her and hopped into the suitcase.

"Can't we get on with this?" Giselle grumbled.

"What's he after?" Camilla asked, quieting the dog. "What's in there?"

Watson pawed at the lining of the suitcase, trying his best to get into a tiny slit cut into one corner. Faith picked him up so the chief could get a better look.

"There is something in here." Garris managed to extract a small vial. Careful not to get his fingerprints on it, he worked the top off and gave it a sniff. There was grim satisfaction on his face. "Ten to one this is our cyanide."

By then Ann had both hands clasped over her mouth. "No. I don't know how that got there, but I didn't do it. I didn't do any of this."

"Oh, Ann," Camilla breathed. "I knew you hated me, but how could you have done this to Jenny? She never hurt you. She never hurt anyone. Whatever you meant to do to me, how could you let your bitterness over my husband make you kill an innocent young woman?"

Ann's lips trembled. "I'm not the one who's bitter about Sterling. You are. And you know why."

Giselle stared at her mother, obviously waiting for her response.

"This is too horrible." Camilla sobbed, holding Emma tighter. "Too horrible."

"You say you didn't know this was here," Garris said to Ann.

She nodded.

"You guys didn't find any kind of medication, did you?" Garris asked Tobin and Laddy. "Something for a headache maybe?"

Both officers shook their heads.

The chief faced Ann. "Did you give the young woman something when she wasn't feeling well?"

"No, I didn't even know Jenny wasn't feeling well."

"She told me that she had a headache," Tony offered. "But she said it was from everything that was happening tonight. I assumed it was nerves."

"None of you gave her anything?" the chief pressed.

Everyone denied having done so.

"Oh," Camilla breathed. "Oh no." She sank suddenly into the chair beside the bed.

"What is it?" Giselle asked. "Mom?"

"Jenny couldn't have. No, she couldn't have."

"Couldn't have what?" Faith asked.

Ralph put one hand on Camilla's shoulder. "What is it?"

"I hadn't thought of it before," Camilla said, her voice low and shaky. "But Jenny was always in charge of my pills. For allergies and everything else. What if she left the ball and came up to my room to get one of my headache pills? What if she took one that someone had poisoned, meaning it for me?"

"Did she typically take your medications, ma'am?" Garris asked.

Camilla shook her head rapidly. "I never suspected it, but Jenny might have helped herself to them off and on over the years without me knowing about it. Why did she have to do that?" she wailed.

Giselle knelt beside her mother's chair, trying to soothe her.

"Maybe we'd better go to your room, Ms. Courtenay," the chief said, "and have a look at those pills."

Watson patted the suitcase lining once more for good measure and then leaped to the floor.

Garris closed the suitcase and gave it to Tobin. "Better put that in the squad car."

20

"There," Camilla said, pointing out the bottle of analgesic capsules next to her bathroom sink.

Chief Garris opened the bottle and sniffed the contents. "I can't say for sure until it goes to the lab, but I bet this is what she took. Obviously you haven't taken any of this, Ms. Courtenay."

"No, but it would have been only a matter of time." Camilla sighed. "Oh, Ann."

"This doesn't seem right to me." Faith gave the chief an apologetic look. "I'm sorry. I'm not trying to do your job, but all three of the finalists have some kind of incriminating evidence against them. It's too obvious."

"I don't know," Garris said thoughtfully. "It seems all three might have reasons for doing away with Ms. Courtenay."

"Not me," Melanie protested. "I never saw her before this week."

"But you want to take her place at Northanger," Giselle said. "You've said so to anybody who'd listen."

"Don't be ridiculous. That doesn't mean I'd kill her because of it. And doing so wouldn't automatically put me in her place."

"Have you been in this room before now?" the chief asked her.

Melanie's eyes widened, but she shook her head.

Garris looked at Ann and Alex. "Either of you?"

They both replied in the negative.

"All right," Garris said. "As far as these pills are concerned—"

"Mel?" Tony said.

Melanie turned to Tony, looking scared now.

"Mel, you have to tell them," he insisted.

"Tony—" Melanie broke off. With a steadying breath, she faced the chief. "Okay, yes, I was in here earlier today before lunch. The door wasn't locked, and I was inside for only a second or two."

"And why was that?" Garris asked gravely.

"I noticed my synopsis had a typo in the first paragraph," she said miserably. "I just wanted to replace the page. You can look in my trash if you want. I tore up the old one and threw it away."

The chief nodded at Tobin, who went to check.

"Tony saw me coming out and asked what I was doing," Melanie went on. "I swear that was all. I didn't want Camilla and Ralph to think I didn't know the difference between t-h-e-r-e and t-h-e-i-r. It's so easy to type the wrong thing and not see it when you proof your work."

"Is that right?" Garris asked Tony.

"It's true. I saw her coming out of Camilla's room when everyone else was downstairs. She told me about the corrected page."

The chief narrowed his eyes. "You didn't believe her?"

"I did," Tony said, turning to Melanie. "I do. I wouldn't have spoken up, but I didn't want it coming out later and looking like something worse than it was. I'm sorry, Mel."

Melanie gave him a tentative smile. "I should have admitted it right off. But I was scared."

"You wanted to take Ms. Courtenay's place at her publishing house," Garris said. "Is that right?"

"Yes, I said that, but I didn't mean anything criminal. I only wanted everyone to know I was going to do my best to win this contest and become a best-selling author." Melanie lifted her chin. "Look, I come from money. People think that can buy everything, and I'm not saying it's not a great advantage, but it can also make people think you can't do anything without it."

"People make a lot of assumptions," Tony said quietly.

"My parents have a good deal of influence in many circles," Melanie admitted. "They could have paid to have my books printed and distributed. But I wanted to make it on my own to prove I was good enough. If I had to cheat or, for some weird reason, kill to win this contest, that would defeat the purpose, wouldn't it? I want people to see that I actually have talent on my own. I want them to see me and not just my family name." She looked pleadingly at Tony. "Can you understand that?"

He nodded, and there was a sympathetic understanding in his eyes that hadn't been there before. "I know exactly what you mean."

More than you know, Melanie, Faith thought.

"It's here, Chief," Tobin said, coming back with Melanie's trash basket.

"Bag that up with the rest," Garris said. "We'll have a good look at it in a while." Then he turned to Alex. "What about you? You had this receipt for peanuts in your pocket. Why would you want to kill Ms. Courtenay?"

"I didn't."

"No reason at all, eh? No hard feelings over anything?"

"I was seeing her daughter. We were talking marriage and everything. Giselle started to believe I was using her to get my book published. I figured that was her mother talking, but I backed off as she asked me to."

Giselle watched him with remorseful, tear-filled eyes.

"Earlier we made up, and I thought maybe we were on the right track again," Alex went on. "But I guess all this has ruined everything. If that little scrap of paper makes her think I'm a murderer, then I don't suppose we have anything left to talk about."

A tear slipped down Giselle's cheek, but she instantly wiped it away, saying nothing.

"And you?" Chief Garris asked Ann. "What's this about Ms. Courtenay's husband?"

Ann motioned to Camilla. "Ask her. She's the one making the accusations. Whatever happened between us twenty-five years ago is old news. I have too much I want to do with my life without carrying around extra baggage."

"And how do you think that vial of cyanide got into your suitcase?"

"I don't know. But like Faith said, it seems odd that you found a piece of incriminating evidence on each of us. I'd say all of it was planted."

"Oh yeah? And why do you think that is?" Garris asked.

"If I were writing it in a book, it would be because the real culprit had put it there."

"I think she's right," Faith said. "None of it fits together. Why would any of them keep the things you found, Chief? And none of them has motive to want to kill anyone else."

"It doesn't make much sense," Wolfe agreed. "All of these items could have been easily disposed of instead of left around so somebody could find them."

Faith nodded. "I think we've been focusing too much on the finalists when these attempts on Camilla's life might have nothing to do with the contest."

"What do you mean?" Camilla asked. "Who else would have a grudge against me?"

"I've been trying to figure out who would," Faith said. "Who might have had a score to settle? Who might have had a lot of time away from everyone else? Who could have had access to Camilla and her room without anyone noticing?"

Camilla's brow wrinkled, and she shook her head faintly. "I don't understand."

"The day after everyone arrived, Giselle came into the library to get some books. She told me about her and Alex. She told me how you had convinced her to break up with him, Camilla, and then she told me how much she cared about him and was afraid she'd lost him forever."

"Yes, I said that." Wide-eyed, Giselle looked at her mother and then at the chief. "I was upset about Alex. I was stupid to break up with him and not even talk to him about what I was afraid of, but that doesn't mean I'd try to hurt anyone. Certainly not my own mother."

"You spent a lot of time in your suite too," Faith said. "No one would have even considered that you might be somewhere else. Maybe tampering with a lamp or rigging a trip wire?"

"No."

Alex rushed to Giselle's side. "Look here, Faith, I don't appreciate what you're implying and—"

"Maybe putting something in her headache pills?" Faith pressed.

"No." Giselle's face was bright red now. "I never did any of those things. Mother, you can't believe any of that. It isn't true!"

Camilla stared at her.

"Maybe you'd better come along with me to the station, Miss Courtenay," the chief said, moving to take Giselle's arm. "We'll get this all straightened out."

"No," Giselle whispered. "No."

Alex moved between her and Garris, glaring at Faith. "She wouldn't have done this! You can't—"

"You can't," Camilla said at the same time. She rubbed her eyes, blotting away the tears, and lifted her chin. "You can't arrest her. She didn't do any of this. I did."

There was a collective gasp.

"You knew," Wolfe said to Faith, his voice low, as everyone else talked at once.

She nodded. "It was the only thing that made sense. I didn't realize it until right now. Those pills—"

"I wasn't going to let you have my daughter arrested," Camilla told Faith, and then a mockery of a smile touched her lips. "I suppose that's what you were counting on."

"I'm sorry," Faith said. "I didn't understand it until now. All those little clues left with the finalists. It was too thorough. Too convenient.

And nothing that happened to you was that serious. All of it could have been serious, but it wasn't, because you hadn't planned for it to be. Not until you poisoned those pills."

"I . . ." Camilla squeezed her eyes shut, fighting for control of her tears and her voice. "I never meant for anyone to take those. They were only supposed to be more evidence that someone was trying to kill me."

Ralph gaped at her. "Why? What would make you do such a thing?"

Camilla had the grace to look ashamed. "Publicity. Readers have moved on to vampires and zombies and serial killers and I don't know what else. My sales have been flagging, and I know you want to find another author to take my place at Northanger Press."

Ralph shook his head. "I've never wanted that."

"I thought if I had something the press could latch on to, it might improve my numbers." Camilla bit her lip. "And I thought if I implicated all the contestants, no one could actually be charged with anything. I didn't think it would cause any harm. And poor Jenny, she never complained. Maybe she always helped herself to my pills when she needed them. They weren't prescription, and they weren't expensive. She probably didn't think anything of it. I've always made it clear to her that she was to make herself at home with me."

"Mother," Giselle breathed, clinging to Alex's arm, "you couldn't have."

"Then I panicked when I realized what had happened," Camilla said stiffly. "I had to blame it on someone."

"So you picked me." Ann sighed. "After all these years, you could never forgive me, could you?"

"The part about Ms. Courtenay's husband, is it?" the chief asked. "I assume one of you took him from the other."

"Sterling and I were going to get married," Ann said with the acceptance that came only with time. "He ended up marrying her."

"Then shouldn't you be the one forgiving her?"

"I have," Ann said simply.

"Then what would she—?"

"Because he loved *her*." Camilla's eyes blazed. "He always loved her, not me. He only married me because of—" She glanced at her bewildered daughter and then looked away. "The baby."

There was complete silence in the Jane Austen Suite.

Camilla reached out to Giselle. "I'm sorry, honey. I'm so sorry. Your daddy loved you. He did. You know he did. And he was good to me. He never threw it in my face about what happened. It was over between us before he fell in love with Ann."

Giselle turned away and pressed her face into Alex's shoulder.

Camilla let her outstretched hand drop to her side, then glared at her rival. "Yes, he loved you. Always. I could see it in his eyes when he talked about you. That look was never there for me, even after we'd been married for years. But when I told him about the baby, he wanted to do the right thing."

As usual, Ann's expression was merely cool.

"I know I should have let him go," Camilla said, as if she had rehearsed this conversation a million times over the past twenty-five years. "But I didn't want to." She regarded her daughter, agony in her eyes. "I planned to have a baby so he couldn't leave me. I wanted him to see how much I loved him. I wanted him to realize I was the one who could make him happy. I tried and I tried, but all along I was wrong. No matter what he said, I knew I was wrong."

Again, there was silence. Giselle still clung to Alex. Dressed in their finery, they resembled a couple from one of Camilla's books. But those were all happier stories than this one.

Camilla turned to the chief. "If you'll allow me a moment," she said, sounding as if all her emotion had been spent, "I'll get dressed." She rummaged in one of the drawers for a few things and then took Emma into the bathroom with her and locked the door.

"I think that'll do for tonight," Chief Garris announced. "If we need more information from any of you, we'll be in touch."

"What will happen to Camilla?" Ralph asked. "She never meant for anything like this to occur."

"I don't know," Garris said. "That'll depend on the DA. She didn't actually give anyone poison or intend for anyone to take it. That ought to be in her favor."

Giselle sniffled and lifted her head. "Could I talk to her for a few minutes before you go?" She glanced at Alex. "Will you wait for me outside?"

He nodded. "I'll wait."

Ralph patted Giselle's shoulder. "You tell her Northanger will stand with her too, okay?" He glanced toward the closed bathroom door and then left the room.

Alex, Tony, and Melanie went with him.

"I never would have wanted this for her," Ann said before she walked out, and there was genuine pity in her dark eyes. Camilla's victory over her, getting the man they both loved, had truly been an empty one.

The chief stayed inside the room with the two officers stationed outside Camilla's door, giving Giselle the few minutes she had asked for.

Faith and Wolfe left and walked down the corridor.

Watson appeared and trotted beside them.

"Where were you just now?" Faith asked, picking him up. "Taking in the whole show, I suppose."

Wolfe scratched behind the cat's ears. "He was a big help in getting all this straightened out."

Watson looked smug.

They were in the lobby by then, and Wolfe showed every sign of expecting to walk her and Watson to their door. She was certainly not going to object to being escorted by a handsome gentleman in exquisite evening wear, but she didn't want to keep him long if he was as exhausted as she was. Neither of them said anything as they walked through the topiaries toward the cottage.

"When I found out about what happened with Ann and Camilla and Camilla's husband," Faith said, breaking the companionable silence as they reached the door, "it struck me that it was the basic story line in *A Love Abandoned*, with the man being forced to marry someone, forced to leave behind the woman he wanted, and then falling in love with his wife after all. But then I realized that must have been how Camilla wishes it had turned out. She couldn't have dreamed things would end up this way. With Jenny and everything."

"Poor Jenny and poor Camilla." Wolfe rubbed behind Watson's whiskers, looking thoughtful. "I hope they'll go easy on her, though even if they decide not to prosecute, I can't imagine how hard it will be for her to live with what she's done. I hope her daughter will support her through this ordeal."

Faith fished her keys out of her reticule and unlocked the door. "I think she will. Ralph too." She allowed herself a tired smile. "It's always nice to have good people to work with."

"I couldn't agree more," Wolfe said, and then he touched Watson's pink nose.

Watson swatted playfully at his hand.

"You two have a good night's sleep," Wolfe said. "I'm sure we'll find out more in the morning."

"Good night." Faith watched him walk back toward the manor until he vanished into the trees.

Saturday morning saw Faith making her way to the manor to see if there was anything else she could do to help before everyone from the contest left.

Watson had elected to stroll along beside her, and he was unusually vocal as they made their way to the manor.

"Yes, I know we couldn't have done it without you," she told him as they went through the front door. "Even Wolfe said so."

The cat looked quite pleased with himself and darted ahead to settle into an overstuffed chair near the front desk.

The group was in the lobby checking out, with their baggage ready to be loaded into the van for the trip to the airport. Camilla was not with them.

"She's still being questioned, I suspect," Marlene whispered to Faith. The look of disdain on her perfectly made-up face could have been spotted from a mile off.

Faith didn't respond. Instead, she walked away from Marlene and joined the others. "How are things this morning?" she asked Ralph.

He managed a slight smile. "All right enough. Camilla is still at the station, but the chief just called to let me know they're letting her go home for now. The district attorney doesn't think she's much of a risk to do anything like this again. That's not to say there won't be some kind of charges brought, but exactly what they'd charge her with, civil or criminal, they haven't decided yet. Anyway, we'll pick her up on the way."

"I'm sorry about everything that happened. It's so sad."

Ralph nodded. "We'll get Camilla through it, but I wish she hadn't thought she had to do this. We had no intention of letting her go. Yes, her sales have dipped recently, but that doesn't mean they won't pick up again. They always have. And if it weren't for her, Northanger would've folded some years ago, but she pushed herself and got us extra books to keep us afloat. We're not going to abandon her now."

"I'm glad to hear it," Faith said. "What about Giselle?"

"I think she'll be all right, but it's hard to say. Maybe you'd better see for yourself."

Giselle was standing by the luggage, holding Emma and talking to Alex, but she broke off when she saw Faith headed toward her.

Seeing the dog, Watson slunk over to Faith and peered around her legs, but neither Emma nor Giselle seemed to notice.

"Faith, I'm so glad you're here." Giselle looked as if she had only recently stopped crying, but she seemed calmer than Faith had ever seen her. "I wanted to thank you for letting me talk to you and for getting all this straightened out." She glanced at Alex. "We're going to stand by Mother, no matter what happens."

Alex nodded.

"I think we'll both understand her better now," Giselle said, cuddling the dog close. "Now that we know everything."

"I'm glad," Faith said. "I hope you'll stay in touch."

There was a hint of a smile on Giselle's lips. "We will."

"Please tell your mother I wish her well," Ann said as she approached. "I know this must be very hard for her." She handed Giselle her business card. "If she ever wants to get in touch, there's my information."

"Did you tell Faith the news?" Tony said as he and Melanie joined them.

Faith lifted one eyebrow. "News?"

Melanie flashed a brilliant smile. "Ralph's giving all three of us a contract. Only one book each, but he says that way the readers can be the ones to decide if any of us go further."

"That's great," Faith said. "After everything that's happened, I think that's the best way to do it. I'm curious, though, about which one of you Camilla chose."

Tony nodded at Melanie, looking fondly proud. "Melanie."

Melanie shrugged. "I have a feeling that was just because I was the only one she didn't have something against."

Alex snorted.

"There was no way she could have known whose was whose," Ann reminded her. "Don't sell yourself short."

"I think I like it Ralph's way better," Melanie continued. "Let the public decide. I'm up for it. At least if I make it big, I'll know I made it on my own."

"I knew we had a lot in common," Tony said with a sly look at Faith.

"I think you do," Faith said. "I hope the two of you have a chance to tell each other about yourselves." She looked significantly at him. "Family and all that."

"Oh, we've been over it," Tony said. "We had a good long talk last night."

Melanie took his arm. "And one day, I hope I get to meet this formidable aunt he told me about." She lowered her voice to a confidential whisper. "Until then, I know how to keep a secret."

"Okay, everyone," Ralph said when he'd finished at the front desk, "we need to hurry if we're going to make our flights. Tony, you have the gate numbers?"

"Yes. Right this way."

Faith watched the two couples follow Ann and Ralph out of the manor, Alex with his arm around Giselle, Tony and Melanie hand in hand. Somehow, even after everything that had happened, both pairs had ended up looking toward a future together. Maybe Aunt Eileen was right and it wasn't too late for her either.

"It's been quite a week, hasn't it?" Wolfe said, coming up behind her.

She turned to him with a welcoming smile.

He smiled in return, then noticed the cat at her feet. "Good morning, Watson."

Watson blinked at him.

"I was disappointed that we never actually got to have the ball," Faith said.

"Me too," Wolfe admitted. "I didn't have the opportunity to ask you to dance."

She looked up at him, trying hard not to blush.

He gave her that slow smile that always made her heart skip a little beat. "I'll make it up to you, mademoiselle." He took her hand, bending over it with a suavity that would have won the approval of any of Camilla's dashing heroes. "Very soon, I hope."

Watson began to purr.

Clearly he agreed.